Fic McGuane, Thomas.   9429
McG Keep the change

WITHDRAWN

DATE DUE

MAR 1 1990 FEB 2 2002		
MAR 14 1990 FEB 2 2002		
APR 19 1990 APR 15 2003		
JUN 15 1990		
OCT 18 1990 MAR 2 0 '08		
JAN 24 1992		
JUN 23 1994		
JUL 8 1994		
JUL 19 1994		
NOV 0 8 1999		
NOV 29 2000		

D1024913

Hailey Public
12 West Carbo
Hailey, Idaho 83333

KEEP THE CHANGE

KEEP THE CHANGE

Thomas McGuane

Houghton Mifflin / Seymour Lawrence
Boston

Copyright © 1989 by Thomas McGuane
ALL RIGHTS RESERVED

For information about permission to reproduce selections from
this book, write to Permissions, Houghton Mifflin Company,
2 Park Street, Boston, Massachusetts 02108.

Library of Congress Cataloging-in-Publication Data

McGuane, Thomas.
    Keep the change / Thomas McGuane.
      p.   cm.
    ISBN 0-395-48887-7
    I. Title.
  PS3563.A3114K44 1989 89-30996
  813'.54—dc19 CIP

Printed in the United States of America

D 10 9 8 7 6 5 4 3 2

Book design by Ann Stewart

For Laurie

4429 pur 2440

I photographed you with my Rolleiflex.
It showed your enormous ingratitude.

ANTONIO CARLOS JOBIM

KEEP THE CHANGE

When Joe Starling was ten years old, his father's bank foreclosed on a fieldstone mansion which was by then a depressing ruin standing by itself in the middle of a fourteen-section cattle pasture. It had been built during the silver rush to house the man who found the vein of ore, but now its mortared walls sheltered cattle against the prevailing west wind. Twenty years later, Joe could not remember much of the house beyond its size and age, and its air of having seen things. Once or twice while he was growing up, he drove over from his family's ranch. He recalled rumors of two old sisters who once lived there, nieces of the Silver King, whose poverty did not prevent them from seeming to have come from a higher caste than other people in the county. The sisters had not been long dead when Joe and his father first visited the house to view a painting that hung over the cavernous fireplace. It was a picture of a range of white hills. At first glance, it had looked like an unblemished canvas until the perplexity of shadows across its surface was seen to be part of the painting.

The picture had been made in the cold part of the year. It

was supposed to have been painted long ago on the upper Missouri River. Joe believed that it was a picture of the hills by someone who feared he would never get out of them. But when he looked at the picture with his father, craning his neck to see up into the shadows, his father said, "It must have faded. There's nothing left."

"It's still a beautiful picture," said Joe.

His father turned and smiled down at him. "Yes, it is," his father said.

Joe had come to believe that he understood what the painter had intended and that it was still right there, perfectly clear. That it had faded only enlarged the force of its mystery. The two old sisters were buried in the yard in graves deep below the frost where coyotes could never reach them, and his father was now in a grave of his own on the edge of a suburban golf course in Minnesota where coyotes never ventured. Cattle had seized the mansion altogether for the purpose of escaping storms and drifting snow. It seemed even more important that a painting unseen by anything but bats hanging in the pine-smoked shadows of the big room disclose its meaning once and for all. When his own picture *Chain-Smoking Blind Man* had become known, only he was aware that its variegated white surface served against the canvas with a number-five putty knife was nothing more than his memory of the faded white hills on walls belonging to the long-dead Silver King and his spinster nieces. The feeling that he had invented nothing and that his career had begun with an undiscovered plagiary was disturbing. It was even more disturbing before he quit painting. Now that Joe was living little better than hand to mouth, the story of the plagiarism seemed part of a stranger's biography.

•

Not long after the visit to the deserted house, Joe's father had been transferred from his job as agricultural vice president of their local bank to a bigger job at the bank headquarters in Minneapolis. And it was there Joe's folks lived forevermore or until they died, neither more nor less happy, but, it had to be admitted, closer to if not their dream, then their view of things. The ranch had been leased to the neighbors, the Overstreets, but the house was available to Joe and so was a summer job of cowboying under the neighbor's foreman, Otis Rosewell, a tight-mouthed Baptist cowboy from Circle. This arrangement prevailed more or less successfully for a few years until Joe came home from his last year in military school in Kentucky, that is, came back to the ranch.

The lessees had but one obligation above and beyond an annual payment adjusted to the fall shipment of cattle, and that was to house up to four English pointers, the health and condition of which were guaranteed in writing by penalty clauses in the lease agreement. Retaining a sporting connection to the property enabled Joe's father to make his annual inspection tours from the gentlemanly stance he now required. The dogs, kenneled for the banker's occasional appearances, generally ran wild, their noses polished off to pink by running in the brush year round and their legs black from excursions through the swamps. But Joe's father was a superior dog handler and within a day or two of hunting in the fall, he usually had them "hitched up" once again, popping along, brightly under control, in search of prairie chickens. Joe remembered this wonderful string of dogs as his father's great pride, especially Neuritis and Neuralgia, the liver and white Elhew males his father raised and broke. And he remembered the three family saddle horses, all geldings, whom Joe's mother called Hart, Schaffner, and Marx because they lurked behind the shelter belt with an air of being in business together.

Joe's father accompanied him on his trip back to the ranch. He wore his gray suit buttoned over his still muscular old cowboy's physique and changed in the bunkhouse when they got there. Otis Rosewell accompanied them on their rounds. They started with the dogs and immediately Joe's father found something to complain about. Otis tilted back on his undershot heels and took it in. "When you see one drag its butt on the ground like that, it needs wormed, Otis. They don't do that as a party gag. You with me?"

"It's just having the time," said Otis in a cool voice and managing to tilt his head so that his hat brim threw a shadow across his already hard-to-read face.

They saddled some horses and started out across the irrigated ground. "I presume your boss means to prove up like he ought to on this lease and that means maintaining the condition of my ranch," Joe's father said. "You can't have spurge and knapweed go on undisturbed like that if you mean to be on this place a long time"—Joe's father stopped his horse and was pointing an incriminating arm at the edges of an undulating hay meadow—"and one place your irrigator has leached all the nutrition out of the alfalfa leaving his water too long in one spot and another it's burning up. Somebody ought to whip his ass."

"I'm the irrigator," said Otis Rosewell from under the brim.

"Who's supposed to watch you?"

"Nobody don't."

Joe's father jogged his horse right over next to Otis. "If I was your boss, I'd make it clear you were to bust your hump."

"I'm sure that's how you feel, Mr. Starling. But it was in poor shape when you had it to yourself."

4

Joe's father didn't appear to hear him. In fact, he halfway seemed to be talking to himself, muttering away as they rode. ". . . but sometimes a man needs to be afoot to keep from going broke, get down and go to his tasks, instead of posing on the horse no matter how bad off and shameful the farmground is." He turned to Joe. "This ranch is a monument to all I've had to take and I'm not letting anyone run it down."

Joe was startled at how well his father could speak bad English. He knew him best in his guise as a bank executive who, as a self-educated man, took pride in correct speech. In fact, as an agricultural executive, up from loan officer, he was able to create a useful gap between himself and his clients through the improved manner of his speaking. As Joe got older, he was able to read the disciplinary atmosphere by the type of language being directed at him. Buried in his father's life was his original manner, identical to that of the farmers and ranchers who came to him with their hats in their hands. What they didn't know, he often said, couldn't hurt them. He was a coldblooded Westerner at heart.

When the three of them reached the end of the irrigated ground, Joe's father excused Otis Rosewell; he literally said, "You may be excused," and Rosewell started back. Joe and his father made their way up the hill toward the sprawling pastures that lay beyond the rims. They didn't speak for the first and toughest part of the climb. Joe rode along behind his father, who let his horse work his way up through the shale and tough footing on a loose rein. The older man sat straight as a string in his saddle, feet loose in his stirrups with floating grace. The two horses had their noses close to the steep ground in front of them while the big muscles in their rumps jumped and contracted with the struggle. When Joe and his father got over the top, they stopped to let the horses blow. The pastures stretched out in a folding world of grassy hills until they disappeared into the bluing of faraway sky.

"If you ever wind up with the place," said his father, "don't have your horses over here in the spring because it's heck for locoweed. And larkspur too. So don't be putting cattle in here before the grass is really up. In 1959 I took a whole truckful of saddle horses to the canners that got locoed right in this exact spot. But whatever you do, even if you graze it flat and the knapweed and spurge cover it up and the wind blows the topsoil to Kansas, don't let that old sonofabitch Overstreet get it. He tried to break me when I came into this country and he darn near got it done. We get along okay now but his dream is to make his ranch a perfect square and this is a big bite out of his southeast corner." He stopped and thought a moment, staring persistently in front of himself. "And if the worst should happen and I am gone and he gets it from you and makes it square, don't let him get the mineral rights. I can see something like this happening with the land, but if he gets what's underneath he's cut off your nuts and it's the Pope's choir for you, kiddo."

Joe loved the place but he didn't expect or really want to end up on it altogether. If Joe was satisfied by the land in which the ranch was situated, and he loved it pretty much wherever his eyes fell, he never quite understood what that had to do with ownership. Right now it was enough to feel his father's passion for the place and try to speculate about how he went on owning something with such deep satisfaction when it was so far from his home on that golf course in Minneapolis. Joe puzzled over the passion with which his father had made a new life there. His father golfed with enthusiasm in his Bermuda shorts, pounding the ball around the fairways with hostile force, the terror of caddies, shaping the land with

6

his clubs, playing through lethargic foursomes with menace and accumulating large numbers of strokes through his enraged putting. They called him "cowboy" in a way that genially suggested that his skills were not suited to civilized life.

As Joe followed his father down the mile-long slope to the main spring he tried to absorb the plain fact that his father meant that this would one day be his. This was not precisely a soaring thought. He really wondered how he would put his heritage in play. He found the future eerie and he already wanted to paint.

The spring lay at the base of the long slope, in a grove of small black cottonwoods and wild currant bushes. It came out of an iron pipe and poured into the end of an old railroad tank car whose thick steel plating and massive rivets made an indestructible water hole that couldn't be trampled into muck the way an undeveloped spring could by cows who stayed thirsty and wouldn't travel to feed, beating the grass down where they lay in diminished vigor. Joe's father explained all this to him and made it clear that it was he who had hauled this great railroad tank up the mountain and developed the spring, wheelbarrowing gravel to the trench and laying the collector pipe one blistering summer in the 1940s.

"But it was worth it," he said, "because every cow who ever came here since then got herself a good long drink of cold water." This made the home on the golf course seem even sadder to Joe, the dawn cries of the foursomes on Sunday even more depressing than he had remembered. The hillsides around Joe and his father were speckled with contented-looking Hereford cattle and their spry calves. His father's satisfaction was a simple one, complicated only by the distance his success had produced.

The horses were lathered when at the end of the day they

7

were turned out once again, white lines of sweat gathered at the outlines of the saddles. The horses ran back into their pasture, stretched to shake from end to end, celebrated liberty by rolling in the dust, jumping back up to shake and stretch again. Then they jogged over the hill and out of sight. Joe's father changed in the bunkhouse, and when he came back, carrying a brown briefcase, he was a banker again in an olive green summer suit, a striped tie, and a dapper straw hat.

Joe rode with his father in a rental car to visit his Uncle Smitty and Aunt Lureen. They were his father's brother and sister. It was late afternoon and Lureen would be home from her teaching job. Smitty could always be found at home.

"This is what you call a social obligation," said his father.

"Oh, I like them, Dad."

"They're all yours, son, at least for the summer. I like Lureen and I suppose I should like Smitty better than I do. He's my brother, after all."

The house was three narrow stories tall, with sagging porches on the two upper floors; it was clapboard and painted a pale green that stood out against sky and telephone wires. The scudding spring clouds moved overhead rapidly. When Joe looked at the house, its cheap simplicity reminded him of his modest family origins of city park employees, Democratic party flunkies, mill workers, railroad brakemen, mechanics, grocers, ranch hands. It forever fascinated him that such unassuming people could have been so mad with greed and desire for fame or love. Joe's father was the first and only member of the family to take on the notion of landholding. One uncle had written passionate letters to aborigine women in care of the *National Geographic*. A cousin had lost his dryland farm in a pyramid scheme. A locket his grandmother had worn all her life contained the photograph of a man not known to the family.

Smitty and Lureen were in the doorway, Lureen in a brown suit she had taught in, and Smitty in the checked shirt and beltless slacks that seemed to suggest well-earned leisure. He looked like a commuter.

They got out of the car and Joe's father stormed up the short flight of steps with insincere enthusiasm. He hugged Lureen fiercely and pumped Smitty's thin arm with comradely fervor. Joe stood back smiling until it was his turn for the hugs and handshakes. It was well known that Smitty had great reservations about Joe's father but they didn't show until he greeted Joe with a suspicious squint and wary twitching of his eyebrows.

The visit was a raucous parade behind Joe's father, who thundered through the rooms, refusing Smitty's suggestion of a drink and Lureen's of tea. He borrowed the telephone for a quick call to the bank in Minnesota, then hung up the phone conclusively as though his conversation with the bank had been the end of his conversation with Lureen and Smitty.

"Junior's got to go to work," he said, gesturing at Joe with his straw hat. He bobbed down to kiss Lureen goodbye, then shot his hand out and let Smitty walk over and shake it. "We'll call you Christmastime!" he thundered and got around behind Joe, pushing at his shoulder blades until the two of them were out on the street and a very strained Smitty and Lureen were waving at them. "You can't have a drink with Smitty without having to go his bail that night."

As they drove, his father said, "Can you imagine a grown man living off his spinster sister like that?"

"I thought Smitty had some problem from the war," Joe said.

"Oh, he did, he did. But I was in the same goddamn war. Listen to me, I want to make a long story short. Don't ever take your eyes off Smitty. He's dumb like a fox. Cut Smitty a little slack and he'll take her all."

They drove back out toward the ranch. "I wish I could have found a way of staying in this country," said his father. "But any fool can see it's going nowhere. Still, you look at it and it just makes you think, What if? You know what I mean?" Joe was so startled by what for them was a rare intimacy that he looked straight down the road and waited for his stop. He thought he knew exactly what his father meant. What if.

Joe's father dropped him at the Overstreet headquarters, next to the tin-roofed granary and saddle shed and bunkhouse where Joe would live for the summer. He leaned over and gave Joe a hug. Joe felt his great body heat and smelled the strong and heartening aftershave lotion.

"Well, son," he said, "it's time to whistle up the dogs and piss on the fire. Have a good summer, and keep an eye on things. You make a hand and they'll have to use you. Then you can watch. Think of it as being yours someday and you'll watch fairly closely."

"Tell Mom hi for me."

"In particular," said his father, "the hay ground. If they

aren't changing water three times a day they're lying to both of us."

All of Joe's father's quirks, including this one of not listening to him closely, only made Joe love him more. He loved the motion of his father, the bustle, the clear goals he, Joe, could not always understand. After all, he was the only father Joe would have and Joe seemed to know that.

Joe was over at the headquarters of the Caywood Fork the next day to get his orders. It was first light and the big riverine cottonwoods that hung over the somber headquarters buildings seemed to hold the last of night in their dense foliage. He had no car for the summer and he'd had to walk. The dogs barked at his arrival and Otis Rosewell came around from behind the saddle shed leading a horse. Joe walked over to him and stopped. Rosewell gazed at him. Finally, a small smile played over his lips.

"Must be tough around your camp," he said.

"What do you mean?"

"Your old man."

"Yes, he is," Joe conceded, wondering in dismay if he was failing some test of loyalty. But he thought Rosewell had extended a small gesture of amiability and he didn't want it to slip away. It could be a long summer.

"Do you know how to run a swather or a bale wagon?"

"No, I don't."

"Can you fence?"

"Sure. And I can run a backpack sprayer, you know, for malathion or whatever."

"Well, most of the fence on your old man's place is falling down because he never took care of it and because it was fenced poorly in the first place. But I imagine he thinks it's perfect and I want you to make his dreams come true because my yearlings are pouring through the sonofabitch like water. Get yourself a pocket notebook and start walking that fence. Pull it up when you can and rebuild it where you have to. Knock out that old crooked cedar and put in some steel. You can get a sledge, stretcher, pliers, post pounder, and staples in the shop and you can use the old Ford to haul it around."

"I'll get started today."

"That's right. And you'll never finish. Now let me tell you something else. You was sent to us. If you don't care to put in an honest day's work, that's your business. I ain't going to hang over you. I work for Mr. Overstreet."

Joe built fence for twenty-one days before he took his first break. He went down all the boundary fence and had five strands of barbed wire on stays sparkling from staple to staple. Where the rotten cedar had given out there were new green-and-white steel T-posts and the soldierly order they gave to the rise and fall of boundaries helped Joe see how his heritage lay on the benign face of the county.

About halfway through his fencing assignment, Joe reached a high divide between two drainages, Crow Creek and Nester Creek. A thousand years of wind had blown all the topsoil to Wyoming and it was just bare rock on top of the world where old barbed wire sang like an Aeolian harp. Otis came up and helped him with this stretch of fence. They started to build jack fence, then changed their minds and dynamited post holes for half a mile until the line pitched down into the woods and was easy again and beyond the eerie sound of the steel strings above them. There was pleasure in working the ratchet on the fence stretcher, watching the wire rise, tighten, and sparkle in the light through the trees, sing in the wind, turn at the corner posts, or drop out of sight over the crown of a hill. Joe was going all round what would one day be his.

On the twenty-first day, he was fencing the bottom of a narrow defile. Cattle had grown accustomed to escaping here by lifting the poles that were meant to hold the bottom wire low. Joe was sewing the fence to the earth along the floor of this cut with a post every ten feet when he was visited by the daughter of the owner, Ellen Overstreet. He had watched her covertly ever since he first got there, mostly when she was riding out through the ranch in the front of a flatbed truck with Billy Kelton, a neighbor Joe hadn't spoken to since a boyhood fistfight almost ten years before. Without any thought of Ellen herself, Joe would have loved to take her away from Billy, who looked so complacent in the truck, lariat hanging in the rear window and his blue-eyed gaze remote under a tall-crown straw hat. It was a grudge.

Joe's first thought was that her timing was perfect. He was dark from the long exposure to sun and the muscles of his arms were hard and defined from driving posts and stretching wire. Ellen was a rangy brunette with startling gray eyes.

"What's the point of this when my dad is going to own it all anyway?" she said with a bright smile.

"I'm getting paid. And I'm here to tell you your dad will never get our place."

"You're getting paid. Otis says you can work or not work, it's no nevermind to him."

"Well, it is to me," said Joe, letting the red post pounder tip over and drop with a clang.

"One way or another, Otis says. He doesn't care."

"You can't go by Otis," said Joe. "If he knew anything he wouldn't be here."

"Otis has been with Daddy since we ranched at Exeter Switch."

"It's not Otis's fault he isn't smart."

Ellen sat down in the deep bluestem and began pulling up the russet pink flowers of prairie smoke, making a bouquet in her left hand and blowing ants off the blossoms.

"Daddy says you're in military school in Kentucky and you're that little bit from graduating and going to Vietnam."

"Only I'm not going to Vietnam. I'm going to college in the East. I'm studying art. Is that for me?"

He reached out for the bouquet of prairie smoke blossoms and she handed them over with a shrug.

"Why aren't we going to Vietnam?"

"Because we aren't supposed to be there in the first place. Everybody knows that."

"Not everybody knows that. A lot of my friends can't wait to get there."

"Well, you've got the wrong friends."

"You better not let them hear your Vietnam theory. I know one or two will fix your little red wagon. We believe in freedom. Y'know Billy Kelton?"

"Yeah, I know Billy."

"Well, he plans to go quick as he can get shut of school."

"That'd be about right for Billy."

"Did you know he was top five saddlebronc rider in the Northern Rodeo Association two years in a row?"

"Nope."

"He's about as pretty a hand with rough stock ever come out of these parts."

16

"That should just chill the Vietcong," said Joe.

Joe wasn't really paying close attention. Almost the only thing he and Ellen had in common was that they were both being dunned by the Columbia Record Club. He was trying to see what she had in the way of breasts. If she hadn't wanted that noticed, she could have bought the right shirt size.

"Otis said you really know how to work."

"He did?" Joe practically sang.

"That seems to mean quite a little to you."

"Not really."

She scrutinized him. He was at a loss for words. The very sound of air seemed to increase. She took a deep breath. "What bands do you like?" she asked.

"The Stones. What about you?"

"The Byrds." On the word "Byrds" he sensed his opportunity and reached to take her hand. It felt small to him, though it was hard to notice anything more than the nervous energy pouring back and forth between them. He would have liked to announce that he was going to kiss her or that he was attracted to her, which he was. But anything which contained much meaning would have subjected him to overexposure. Nevertheless, for things to continue, it was necessary that he express something about the moment. He said, "Oh, wow." To his immense relief, "Oh, wow" was very acceptable. Ellen Overstreet seemed to melt very slightly at these less than eloquent words. "I mean it," Joe added and took the other hand.

"What are you taking?" she breathed, her face angled down at the ground between them.

"Algebra, History, Spanish, English. What about you?"

"Soc. Home Ec. Comm Skills. Phys Ed." Joe wasn't thinking so much about her courses. He could tell that she was looking to him for leadership. That he knew next to nothing, probably no more than she, didn't matter because he had arrived from out of state and his real background was lost behind this ripped T-shirt, these new muscles, and this tan. He drew Ellen to him and kissed her. Feeling the hard line of her clamped lips, he realized that Ellen was ready to be kissed but didn't know much more than to lean face forward. It might take all summer to get those lips open.

They went on kissing. A couple of times, she had "thoughts" as she called them that made laughter burst through her nose. Joe waited grimly for these "thoughts" to pass and went back to the awkward business of kissing and hugging. He had numb spots from the rough ground, and any attempt to get "more comfortable" as he explained it, that is, to lever Ellen into a reclining posture, failed miserably. Finally, she detached herself and got up.

"Well, it's nice to meet you, Joe. We'll have to do something one of these days."

"That'd be great," he said, quite certain he knew what she meant by "something."

"Like maybe we could ride on Saturday."

"Oh, wow."

When she started to leave, he gave her the peace sign. His best friend back at school, Ivan Slater, said day in and day out you could get familiar with strange girls faster by using the peace sign as a greeting than any other way.

But Ellen, seeing his raised fingers, said, "Two what?"

Joe just shook his head.

"The two of us?" she said. "Oh, you're sweet!"

Joe and Otis crossed paths as two professionals, and Otis had taken to questioning Joe about little things he was noticing, the levels of springs, the appearance of yearlings that had had diphtheria, pink eye, cancer eye, bag problems, warbles. Joe renewed the fly rubs up in the pasture and ran the chute when Rosewell had cattle in to doctor. He had gotten so he knew all the levers of the headcatch, the catch itself, the gate, the squeeze. He knew which bars to flip out on the cattle they had missed branding so that they could get old man Overstreet's 9-Bar on the left hip. At first, it disturbed Joe to watch the irons smoke into flesh, and the tongue-slung bawling of the cattle as pain drove manure down their back legs. In the end, he turned the irons over in the fire himself to get the right pitch of heat, to make sure the brands went on bright and clean. He quit noticing when the burning smell drifted on the summer air. And to make up for it, he doctored the ones that had eye ulcers from burdocks in the hay they had been eating.

Not long after Joe and Ellen had started to see each other,

he was asked up to the Overstreet house. It was an old two-story ranch house with a dirt path beaten from the driveway to the entry. With ill-concealed distaste, small, fat Mrs. Overstreet led Joe to her husband's office, a room off the bedroom where water rights filings, escrow receipts, bills, brand inspections, road permits, cattle registries, breeding and veterinary records, defunct phone books, memorandum pads, and calendars were heaped up on a rolltop desk. Mr. Overstreet sat on a kind of spring-loaded stool that permitted him to swivel around, tilt back, and regard Joe all in one movement. He was nearly as small as his wife and in every gesture he radiated a lifetime of sharp trading. Like many old-time ranchers, there was nothing "Western" about him. A topographical map on the wall illustrated the boundaries of the ranch. He went to it and pointed to the large missing piece on the south side. "See that?" His eyes burned at Joe. They seemed to consume the papery little face that curved up under a halo of thin iron-gray hair.

"Yes, sir."

"That belongs," said Overstreet, "to you people."

"Yes, sir."

"It spoils the shape of this other, don't you think?"

Joe said nothing.

"Besides that, I'd like to hear how you're getting along. In your own words."

"I'm getting along fine."

"Your salary comes out of my lease arrangement with your daddy. So I'm not out there wringing the last penny from your hide. I do that mainly with Otis. But he says we're getting our money's worth." He removed his glasses and worked his thumb and forefinger into his eye sockets as he spoke. He turned his gaze to the map of the ranch and restored his glasses.

"Joe," he said, "you come from the big wide wonderful world out there. Ellen comes from right here on this little bitty patch of ground. Now no more than I'd try to sell you a pasture without water, don't you sell Ellen something she really isn't in a big way of needing. You catch my meaning?"

"I guess I do."

"You do, Joe. Take it from me. You catch my meaning. Now go on out and keep doing the good job you've been doing. Your dad will be proud of you. You're doing a man's job. If he ever fires you, you come and see me. I'll take you to Billings and teach you to trade fat cattle. I'll teach you to wear out two Cadillacs a year packing cattle receipts. Why, if I had your youth and my brains, I could walk on the backs of my cattle to Omaha. Go on out there, Joe, and *bow your damn back.*"

But Joe didn't get the message exactly. He was stirred instead by the romance of landholding that the old man radiated from his cluttered office. And when he and Ellen returned to their little wickiup in the willows alongside Tie Creek, he was less accepting of the plateau that they had reached weeks before. The wickiup was just a place where they had artfully bent the willows into an igloo shape and lashed them down. Ellen had read somewhere that it was the way the Indians had once sheltered themselves. The wickiup was an easy walk from the house and perfectly camouflaged. They were so secure in this shelter that they calmly went on with their activities even when Otis Rosewell rode past a few yards away. They lapped their tongues while the backs of their heads moved in vague figure-eights. They repeated "I love you" and tried to key their utterances to blissful peaks or reflective sighs. A long silence, a sigh, and an "I love you" indicated they had foreseen an extensive future with all its familiar appurtenances and had taken the phrase "I love you" as a kind of shorthand. Joe ached with meaning. Ellen undid the metal snap in back of her brassiere and her breasts were revealed. Either he would sweep his hand slowly up her rib cage and encompass them, or he would unpack them carefully. They were full handfuls with graceful small nipples. And once when Ellen was doing a handstand, Joe made out the faint blue veins underneath. No matter what position Ellen was in, they stuck straight out. If he mashed them gently, they resumed their perfect shape upon release. If he pushed them to one side and let go, they sprang back. They were practically brand new and the feeling Ellen insisted upon was that they were so wonderful they canceled any further expectations.

Joe overflowed with feeling for the girl in his arms. He had never felt such strong emotions. Everything meant something bigger. He could look at her for hours from only a couple of inches away.

Together Joe and Ellen began to adopt the mopey love-struck postures, the innocent paralysis of young lovers in small towns. On Saturdays, they took one of the ranch trucks and drove into Deadrock for a swim at the city pool. Instead of yanking at each other and yelling by the poolside, they demonstrated the depth of their feeling by quietly working on their tans in fingertip proximity, or eating quietly by themselves at a shady snow-cone franchise. Joe could accept this because he knew the necessary crisis was coming. Gliding along on these parallel paths, feeling vaguely upset in this atmospheric filigree, watching the others thunder past barefoot at poolside, hot on the heels of screeching females, or crammed in fleshy heaps within sun-scorched automobiles, was almost acceptable to Joe because he was being swept along by something thrilling that he had no interest in understanding.

But when Saturday night came around, Joe watched in astonishment as Ellen rolled out the ranch road in Billy Kelton's flatbed truck. Billy and Joe had been best friends until that day ten years ago when Billy beat Joe senseless. Joe was still not over the sense of injury. For his date with Ellen, Billy hadn't even removed the stock rack or taken his saddle out of the bed. His filthy old chaps, lashed to the crosspiece behind the cab, flapped away carelessly. "That sumbitch must be harder than hell to steer," Joe shouted as they went past waving, "the two of you having to sit under the wheel like that!"

But the truck came back up the road at ten. Joe saw them through the bunkhouse window. He had been pacing around, expecting to be up half the night. He dove to extinguish his light. In a short time, Ellen tapped at his door.

"Who is it?" Joe called.

"Ellen. Can I come in?"

Joe conquered the wish to let her in. "I've got a lot to do tomorrow."

"Joe, I've got something to tell you."

"Tell it to the Marines. Tell it to Billy Kelton. I think you two should be very happy together."

She cried outside the door for a while. Finally, she said, "Good night," and Joe fell asleep.

Otis Rosewell generally stayed in town with his wife, but when things ran late, he bunked with Joe. He and Joe had a nice, easygoing relationship based on Joe's looking up to Otis, and admiringly asking for advice. One night when they were musing about cows and horses and smoking cigarettes, Otis tossed an old screwdriver in his hand as he told about an older cowboy he knew who had worked for the Padlock and for Kendricks' in Wyoming; this man, Otis claimed, would go out by himself for weeks at a time with his bedroll and a lariat and would single-handedly rope, brand, vaccinate, and castrate hundreds of calves. "It took a hell of a horse to keep that rope tight, naturally," Otis went on. "But this old boy slept on the ground with his head on his saddle and hobbled his pony and went from one end of the herd to the other! He was born in a damn hurricane, this feller was — " On the far side of the bunkhouse, a rat ran up out of the woodpile about three feet up the wall. Otis threw the screwdriver toward the woodpile and it turned over in the air and speared the rat to the wall. The rat expired. Joe stared. Otis retrieved his screwdriver, threw the rat out the door and sat down.

"Let me see you do that again," Joe said.

"Run up another rat," Otis said.

When the time came, it came quickly. Joe went, hat in hand, to Mr. Overstreet in his office and, conscious that he was triggering the fall of his daughter's virginity, said, "Mr. Overstreet, I'll be going back to school soon. I think I'll finish up and head out." Word of his imminent departure would speed through the ranch. Awful Mrs. Overstreet would rub her daughter's nose in it. Joe was getting ready to run up another rat.

Overstreet stood in the door of his office, which was dim except where the old gooseneck lamp lit the desk, holding a fountain pen poised in front of his chest, and said, "We'll send your dad a good report. You've been a great deal of use to him and to us. I hope we haven't seen the last of you."

"In case I don't bump into Ellen or Mrs. Overstreet, please tell them how much I have enjoyed the opportunity of being here this summer."

"Well, you'll have to tell Ellen yourself," said Mr. Overstreet. "She's soft on you. Even an old-timer like me can see that. Do this family a favor and let Ellen hear from you once in a while." Joe savored the peculiarity of this departure, the old man contemplating the free labor, himself laying the fuse to carnal dynamite.

Late that afternoon, Ellen flung herself onto the floor of the wickiup and began to weep quietly. Joe hung his head. He wasn't really cynical. He loved Ellen. He'd had the best summer of his life with her. She was like a merry shadow to him, superb with horses, incapable of worry, able to freely get around the back country that surrounded the ranch. She knew all the wild grasses as well as she knew the flowers, and could tell before they rode over a rise if that was the day they would come upon newly bloomed shooting stars or fields of alpine asters that weren't there the previous week. She could spot a cow humped up with illness from literally a mile off, or a horse with a ring of old wire around its foot from even farther. Every walk or ride they'd taken, every middle of the night trip to town made under the noses of her tedious parents, led to this moment.

Joe kissed Ellen through her tears and began to undress her. With a languorous and heartbroken air, she helped him until finally she slid her jeans down over her compact hips. She was nude and Joe thought his heart would burst. There was a baffling mutual tragedy in this nudity. He got undressed. He had never known air in such cool purity. The air around them and between them had a quality it could never have again. When he took Ellen in his arms, her absolute nakedness was such a powerful thing it frightened him. He had to return to familiar kissing, familiar strokes of her hair to bring things back to dimensions he could absorb and dispel the sense that he had hit some kind of thrilling but finally overpowering wall. He had to collect himself; but when he drew back, Ellen was once again full in view, no longer even sitting up to accommodate his movement, but remaining supine while he cleared his head of voices.

He moved onto Ellen and simply lay atop her with his knees against hers. Gradually, the pressure of her knees gave way and one of his slid between them. She let her legs part so that his knees touched the blanket underneath them. Then he felt her spread her legs. He tried to lift up on his arms to see but she held him strongly and wouldn't let him. He slid his hand between the points of their hips, held himself until he was started inside her, and pushed. He'd only entered a moment before he emptied himself in scalding shudders. He felt lost.

Otis took Joe to the train in Mr. Overstreet's truck. When they got to the station and pulled up in front of the columns, Otis let his eyes follow a porter pushing an iron-wheeled wagon along the side of the tracks. "You take care, Joe," he said over the roar of the wagon wheels. There was a bright September sun shining down on the world.

"I will, Otis. You too."

"I think you done Mr. Overstreet a fine job."

"I appreciate that."

"I'm sure they'd always be work for you if he was to get the place off your old daddy."

"Is that what his plan is?"

"I'd say so, Joe. He don't figure on you to fight for it."

"I'd rather fight for it than come back and work for old man Overstreet."

"He's a cheap sonofabitch," mused Otis. "Well, Joe, we'll be seeing you. And good luck."

No sooner had Otis pulled out and Joe had started dragging his duffel bag toward the passenger cars than Billy arrived in his flatbed with all the stuff still in back and climbed out. He stopped on the gravel and gestured to Joe. He took off his hat and put it back inside his truck. There was a white band of forehead against his sunburned face.

"Come here, you," he said, with his hands on his hips.

Joe didn't want to walk over at all. He felt almost paralyzed with fear but knew he couldn't live with himself if he didn't walk over. This was going to be a fight and Joe didn't know how to fight. Billy had whipped him a decade earlier and it looked like it was going to happen again. He started to walk over, feeling he might turn and bolt at every step. He stared back at Billy, at first out of a doomed sense of duty and then with increasing isolation until all there was before him was the gradually enlarging figure of Billy amid the uproar of the railroad station and town streets. Billy dropped him with the first blow and Joe struggled to his feet. He wasn't upright before Billy slugged him again and Joe himself could hear the fist pop against the bone of his face. As he struggled to his feet once more, he heard a passenger cry out that enough was enough, but now he had Billy by the front of his shirt and was hauling him toward himself. As Billy began to chop into his face with short, brutal punches, Joe saw Billy being pushed back at the end of a policeman's nightstick. The policeman stepped between Joe and Billy. They stared at each other with the dismay of strangers meeting on the occasion of a car wreck. "Good luck in Vietnam," Joe said bitterly. He looked at Billy, who was glassy eyed with hatred, and then Joe turned to head toward the train. When he bent to pick up his duffel, he fainted.

It seemed Joe would always spend plenty of time unraveling misunderstandings with women. The following summer, when he was eighteen, he'd hitchhiked to Mexico and wound up in a small town in Sonora. He remembered cattle trucks going between the adobe walls on the edge of the town and kind of careening around the fountain too fast, like in the movies. He remembered the constant murmuring of mourning doves and the First Communion girls in white clouds in front of the church. He remembered the century plants and ocotillos with their orange blossoms and gaunt cattle that seemed to walk so hopelessly. He remembered a shirtless man standing next to a hanging side of beef, cutting and weighing pieces of meat for passing customers and rolling the pesos nervously around his forefinger. Joe remembered the town being a dusty grid, poor animals carrying things for the poor people, insignificant things to our eyes like bundles of sticks. It made him ashamed to have anything.

He was led by two boys into a cantina and up to a prostitute, a nice-looking girl who was very tall for a Mexican. He went upstairs. She gave herself to him and Joe responded by falling in love with her and spending every effort to think how she could be reformed and taught English so that he could make her his wife. Joe sat all night in the cantina, a shrunken presence, entertaining her and allowing her to peel his roll of pesos like an artichoke. They danced. They arranged to be photographed at their table. When Joe left for the States, he had the picture, the shirt on his back, and a stricken heart.

In the fall, when he was back in school, Joe's mother found the photograph. She was holding it between her two hands, staring at it, when she called him to her room.

"Joe," she said, "I'm *so* ashamed of you." Joe didn't know what to say. Nothing was appropriate. She lifted her eyes until she had him. "Here you are"—she returned her gaze to the photograph—"with this lovely young woman"—she looked up at him in penetrating disappointment—"and *your shirt is out!*"

Joe's mother taught everyone to play bridge, and about this she had a sense of mission. There was some kind of opiated cough medicine available with which she had dosed Joe, aged four, so that his antics would not disrupt the games taking place in front of the big sixteen-pane window that looked out on the low bluffs that still had the bones of buffalo exposed by spring rains. And Joe daydreamed the bridge afternoons away in apparent bliss. His mother played bridge every week, deeply bored by her companions, the lumpish locals. She thought of her fellow Montanans as humped figures limited by the remote flickers of undeveloped consciousness. She had hoped against hope that her son Joseph Starling, Junior would set out and find culture somewhere, uplifting companionship, make a name for himself, and more or less stay out of town.

As an only child, Joe had been most divided by the contrasting claims of his parents. His father still had the Westerner's ability to look into pure space and see possibilities. His mother saw traditional education as a tool for escape, an escape she couldn't think of making but one which her son could somehow make for her.

Joe graduated from the Kentucky Military Institute and to his father's great satisfaction was accepted by Yale. That happiness quickly disappeared at Joe's decision to study art. When Joe's father visited him at Yale and saw displays of student work and, worse, the crazy-looking building where art was taught, he told Joe they would have nothing to say to each other if this kept up. Joe painted landscapes but they were so austere that they approached not being there at all. They deepened his father's suspicion that this was, despite the endorsement of major institutions, a complete swindle.

His conviction was not altered when Joe got out of school, moved to New York, and became a successful painter. Though it was a career, it was apparently not enough of a career. From Joe's point of view, something wasn't sinking in. The next thing was he couldn't paint. It didn't seem all that subtle psychologically; and he had a good grasp of it. He had always painted from memory and for some reason he couldn't seem to remember much of late. He hoped it was temporary but at the moment, he didn't have anything to offer anyone, even the gallery owners who were practical enough and who knew what was called for. He seemed to have folded his tent and that was that.

But before this, before his love of paint and painting deepened to a kind of dumb rapture, his relationship with his mother grew closer. She resumed a long-buried girlishness. Eventually, this closeness applied to more serious matters.

One summer after the family had moved to Minnesota, Joe was staying on the ranch, painting and doing most of the irrigating. His mother, having announced the seriousness of her mission, flew out from Minnesota for a visit.

Joe made iced tea and they went out and sat at a picnic table under half a dozen flowering apple trees; the trees hadn't been pruned in years but sent forth flowers in drenching volume among the dead branches. There was a telephone pole in the middle, which took something away from the scene; and, just beyond, a wooden feed bunk for cattle with four tongue-worn salt blocks. A handful of pure white clouds floated overhead without moving. Joe and his mother had sat right here in the same spot when he was a child discussing sack races, nature, wild flowers, life, anything that came up. His mother still twirled her hair with her left forefinger when she was thinking, while Joe went on lacing his fingers and staring at them until a thought would come. They had always called the desired outcome of events "an amazing voyage," as in "It would be an amazing voyage if you passed physics this term."

"Make a long story short," said Joe.

"It's inherently a long story."

"Try your best."

His mother drank some of her iced tea. She ran her fingers through her hair, pushing her head back to look up in the sky. She made a single click on the picnic table with an enameled fingernail. "Dad is going to have to be dried out. He has had serious problems with his diverticulitis which surgery would cure, but surgery is out of the question because he will go into the DTs before he can recover."

Joe thought for a moment. "Maybe he should just go through the DTs and deal with the rest of it afterwards."

"At his age and in his state, I am assured that he will shake himself to death if he goes into the DTs unless he does it in a clinic."

"Can he live with the diverticulitis?"

"No."

Beyond the orchard, the beavers had dammed a small stream and the cattails had grown up. A dense flock of redwing blackbirds shot out, followed by a goshawk in tight pursuit. The goshawk flared off into a cottonwood and watched the blackbirds scatter back among the cattails. At a certain point, it would start again.

"I have a feeling you can make this story shorter than you're letting on."

"This part I can condense. You have the best chance of getting Dad into the clinic."

Joe leaned one elbow on the table and rested his face on his hand. "Does he even like me, Mother?"

"Not particularly."

"In that case, maybe I do have a chance," he said, as though elated at a glimmer of light. In fact, he was quite wounded. And in the end it was to no purpose.

That summer, Joe's father went bankrupt in Minnesota. But he saw it coming and signed his ranch over to his sister Lureen to protect it from receivers. Speaking directly to Lureen, confirming that conversation in a letter and sending a copy of the letter to Joe, he expressed his intention to one day take the ranch back and finally to leave it to his son Joe. But he never got the chance: He died driving his car to bankruptcy court, a black four-door Buick coasting through Northfield, Minnesota, with a corpse at the wheel. This ghastly scene dominated the local news for a month.

His father had played around with his wills so often that none of them was binding and for all practical purposes, he died intestate. The property in Minnesota went to Joe's mother, and sufficient investments had withstood bankruptcy proceedings that she was able to live comfortably. Lureen never offered to give her the ranch back. She made it clear that she was holding it for Joe. She and Joe's mother had known each other since the days in the two-room Clarendon Creek schoolhouse when they were both girls. They never liked each other. Joe's mother said, "Lureen has been a wall-flower and a cornball since kindergarten." Lureen said Joe's mother had "enjoyed all the benefits of prostitution without the health risks and the forced early retirement." It was the sharpest statement Lureen made in a long, quiet life; and it had so tremendously amused Joe's father that he had repeated it to Joe with delight. To this day, Joe didn't know what to make of it, or know why it had delighted his father, the banker and former cowboy. A year after his father died, his mother died — connected events.

Joe and Lureen had never failed to communicate with per-fect clarity on the matter of the ranch. Lease payments were made to her; she deposited them and sent a check on to Joe. A separate account was opened to compensate Lureen for her increased taxes as well as a management fee for discussing arrangements with the Overstreets once a year. Lureen lived on her teacher's retirement money and on social security. She owned her home and lived in it simply and comfortably. Joe offered to help out with her needs. She didn't seem to want that, and often remarked that she saw it as her mission to properly attend to the business which Joe's father had placed in her hands. At some point, the matter of transferring it into

Joe's name would be taken care of; and that would be that. Unfortunately, Smitty developed pride of ownership.

After a couple of years in New York, Joe moved to Florida where it was always warm, and soon he met Astrid, riding the front of a 1935 Rolls-Royce, wearing nothing but gold spray paint. She was going to a costume party as a hood ornament. When they danced, he got gold paint on his clothes. This much he could remember about their first kiss: the instant it was over, she said, "You're driving me crazy." He had been dating a girl he'd met when he delivered a specimen for his annual physical, a big-voiced Hoosier girl whose tidy apartment was decorated with Guatemalan molas and posters from gangster movies. She didn't stand a chance against Astrid, who went everywhere with a train of dazed men who hated themselves for being so drawn to her. Astrid scalded them with her Cuban laugh or sent them on demeaning errands.

Not long after the costume parade, Joe and Astrid spent an entire evening making death masks and Joe propped his next to his place at the dinner table, and then so did Astrid. She said, "You look incredibly old in your death mask." He had been uncomfortable breathing through a straw.

Joe said, "Yours doesn't look so good itself." He stuck his tongue through the mouth hole of her death mask. "The other thing is, I've got an empty feeling," he said.

After they began living together, Astrid used to ask him why he didn't paint. He asked her, "Paint what?"

After a few years, she quit asking.

To make a living, Joe became a freelance illustrator of operation manuals. This attainment, through his perfect draftsmanship, had at the beginning peculiar satisfactions. He went to work for his old school friend, Ivan Slater, now a successful businessman. Ivan was not interested in art; Ivan was interested in making others understand how things ran. Ivan would tell them how things ran and Joe would show them. He felt he was selling something real. He had nothing more neurotic to concern himself with than meeting deadlines and his vision of people he hadn't met operating diverse gadgets. The big catch with this work was that it always involved Ivan Slater, Joe's most annoying friend, who had failed upward to a considerable personal fortune. Joe wasn't the least bit jealous and was even flattered that Ivan construed it an act of friendship to try to lure him away from what he considered his fairly dopey earlier life.

The first thing Joe showed Americans how to run was a battery-powered folding hair dryer. The former landscapist made the instrument jump out at you, its operating features so vivid as to be immediately understood. On the bright curve of the instrument's side, Joe let the outer world suggest itself in a little glint. Joe poured his heart into the glint. The glint contained tiny details of his ranch in Montana and gave the impression that the hair dryer was right at home in fairly remote circumstances. It made him happy and it in no way impeded the new owner from acquiring knowledge of drying his or her hair. The company comptroller cut Joe a check. Joe went on with his life. The grazing lease allowed him some selection in the jobs he took. Astrid blamed the lease payments for his not painting; she called them his food stamps.

Joe showed people how to operate an electric lazy susan, a garage door opener, an automatic cat feeder, a board game based on geopolitics, a portable telephone so small it could be pinned to one's clothing, a radar detector for cars, and a gas-powered fire log. For a long time, Joe built up his interest in these projects by imagining that he was working for a single prosperous family, five painfully stupid yet happy people who wanted to be able to run this worthless shit they'd paid good money for.

Ivan Slater had consolidated a lot of solid-state and semi-conductor information and come up with a "portable secretary" brand-named "Miss X," a laptop computer powered by batteries, the same size as the average briefcase. Miss X was complicated to use and complicated to describe in that her functions were so diverse—typing, dictation, filing, and more. Ivan Slater was an ingenious technician but a poor salesman, and dragging Joe by the sleeve through the trade shows of a dozen cities, Ivan made the same startling pitch time after time: "Miss X will do everything but suck you off back at the Ramada!" Ivan saw himself as one of the new "hands-on" industrialists, a growing class of powerful men led by the owners of Remington Shaver and Two Thousand Flushes Toilet Cleaner, who appeared in their own television commercials excitedly demanding your business; Ralph Lauren, casting himself as a cowboy in his own print ads; and the king of them all, Lee Iacocca of Chrysler with his immortal "I guarantee it." These men were Ivan Slater's heroes and he did not defer to them in forcefulness.

At a trade show in Atlanta, Joe had an opportunity to taste the resistance among some of his peers which Ivan Slater had generated. They were set up in a booth of their own at a convention center near Peachtree Plaza. The style of their industry was such that a curiously sedate atmosphere prevailed. At an automotive or homebuilders show, it would have been pandemonium. But these were the businesspeople of a new age; restraint and an ambiguously intellectual tone made it a ghostly crowd. Joe stood behind a table upon which rested a mock-up of the laptop secretary. He had a stack of brochures and, since he had not finished the instructional drawings, he was there to explain the machine in his own words. Ivan had long since driven himself into the middle of the crowd.

A man approaching sixty made his way toward the table. He was tall and dressed in a well-tailored gray pin-stripe suit. He stared at Miss X without taking a brochure. His left arm was wrapped around his waist and his right hand held his face as he thought.

At last, he spoke: "Is this the one that does everything but suck your dick?"

"Yes, but we're working on it," Joe said.

A week later, Joe was back in Florida. He called Ivan in New York and admitted that he didn't think he could go on with Miss X.

"Miss X," said Ivan, "is history."

Joe believed that he had lost all control of his fate. He knew he couldn't stand one more liaison with someone with irons in the fire. Whatever it was that had pushed him from one place to another was not going to push him any farther. He couldn't understand why when he looked within as he had done for so long in his apprenticeship, he found nothing he could use.

Within a week, Ivan came to Florida. He took Joe and Astrid to lunch at a restaurant so heavily air conditioned the windows were fogged.

"It goes like this," Ivan was saying. "Miss X was a classic example of *not* actually having an idea, of trying to synthesize what was already out there. And it was a good synthetic but its prospects were limited and, hey, I don't blame you for being bored by it. At its center was a complete lack of originality. To invent Miss X, I had to turn myself into a committee and it showed."

"I gather the reason you're so cheerful is that you have a better idea," Joe said.

"I looked out and asked myself, What is the one thing that most characterizes our world? What one thing? The answer is 'distrust.'"

Astrid said, "That's true."

So Joe said, "It's true."

"I set myself the task of inventing a machine that addressed itself to distrust, that my Chinese friends could make with microcircuitry, and that I could sell grossly marked up by the carload. A man once told me that the perfect product costs a dime to make, sells for a dollar, and is addictive. This is along the same lines."

"What is it?" Joe asked, annoyed by the long buildup.

Ivan lifted his glass. A smile played over his lips as his eyes shot back and forth between Joe and Astrid. "A home lie detector," said Ivan.

"Have you brought it with you?" Astrid asked anxiously.

"Not to worry. It is only a twinkle in my eye. But the projected cash flow on this one looks like a pyramid scheme. It's going to be as universal as television. It's going to shrink white-collar crime. It's going to drive cheating housewives into the streets by the millions. The President and the First Lady will be gangster-slapping each other on the White House lawn after an evening with the product. A worldwide defrocking of priests will stun believers. Fundamentalist preachers will be turned out of their Taj Mahals by the grinning hordes that placed them there. Four officials will remain in Congress, all truthful morons. It will be necessary to staff our hospitals with veterinarians. Farriers will pull teeth. Canned goods will be sold without labels by word of mouth. *America* will stand *revealed.*"

"Will this be difficult to operate?" Joe asked feebly. He felt disgraced as Ivan's stooge.

Ivan massaged an imaginary ball in the air in front of him. His delight at Joe's cooperation was boundless. "Difficult to operate! It's only got two buttons: 'true' and 'false'! It's as simple as the cross they crucified Christ on. It's got everything that's been missing from modern life in two eloquent buttons. By the time this baby makes its third pass through the discount stores, it will have produced a cleansing fire. I mean, the little things! The waiter in Fort Lauderdale who hands you three-week-old cod you ordered as snapper and says 'Enjoy.' I mean, you *follow* the sonofabitch to the kitchen and strap this baby onto him—"

"Wait a minute," said Astrid. "Wait a minute, wait a minute, wait a minute. You can't use this thing like a gun. You can't hook a waiter up to a lie detector while you are ordering in a restaurant."

"You will be able to once society has accepted it," said Ivan with a wounded look.

It was at this point that Joe, and maybe Astrid too, realized Ivan had some problems, that the whole idea was not completely reasonable, any more than Miss X was reasonable, and that what they were seeing here was desperation. In fact, when Joe caught Astrid's worried eye, they managed to communicate that some humoring was in order. And for a moment, they enjoyed the closeness that spotting Ivan's disease implied. Then Joe thought, Maybe they're humoring *me*. Ivan and Astrid had developed what was to Joe a cloying camaraderie, a nauseating chumminess that produced periodic bursts of advice, often directed at Joe.

Ivan felt the awkwardness. His volubility had vanished. "The air is so humid," he said.

"You get used to it," Astrid said, as though interpreting the situation, yet sitting back to watch him handle it.

"What do people do around here?" he asked.

"Oh gosh," Joe said, "the usual things."

"Barbecues?" Ivan asked. He was back in control.

"Oh, no. Much more than that. They have movies and their clubs," Joe said, struggling with each of these replies.

"Clubs? Name a club."

"The Moose."

"The Moose? That's a club?"

"Yes."

"That they go to?"

"Yes."

"Do you go to The Moose?"

"No."

"But what do *you* do, Joe?"

"What do I do?"

"Am I putting too much pressure on you?"

"Not at all," Joe said. "But that question is completely hypothetical."

Astrid lit a cigarette. Now she was watching Joe.

"Hypothetical? 'What do you do?' is hypothetical?" Ivan asked.

"I think it is."

"Joe, *no you don't.*"

"You guys mind if I turn that down?" Joe asked, pointing to the air-conditioning register. He held his throat with his thumb and forefinger, swallowing emphatically. "I'm not sure how healthy those things are, actually."

Now Joe was seated at the end of a bar. There was a ball game on TV. He looked into the bottom of his glass for a big idea. He was sitting with a guy named Mack thinking about the ranch, about Smitty and Lureen, about his childhood enemy Billy Kelton, about Ellen and old man Overstreet, about the hills and all the moving water. It wasn't just nostalgia; the lease money had quit coming in. And he wasn't getting along with Astrid.

"It's a tie game," Mack said, staring over the silhouetted heads at the screen. "You think you'll go up and see who?"

"My aunt and uncle. They live in our old house in Montana. I might just go on up there."

"Call first," said Mack. "They could be dead."

"Don't you ever feel like seeing your relations?"

"I think it's all this roots thing. My kids go out and tape the locals. I must not be the right guy for this one. It's a little off-speed for me. That's three thousand miles!"

Joe went back to the apartment. Astrid had tied her black hair back with a strip of blue cloth. She smiled at Joe. Something was in the air. Astrid was not a worrier and you couldn't make her worry if it didn't really come to her on her own. She looked at him, held his eye. Silence fell over the room. He came over and kissed her slowly. She was sitting in a chair at the end of the dining table and he was standing over her, kissing her. She undid his pants and held him. When he stopped kissing her, she took him inside her mouth. He had one hand on the back of her head and supported himself with the other on the table. The mail was piled there and most of it was bills. He tried not to acknowledge that he had seen the bills but it was impossible, there were so many of them. He moaned and she sucked harder. He looked at the gas bill. Knowing it would be enormous, he moaned with particular feeling. She gripped his buttocks with both hands and tried to take him in farther. He shuffled the mail with his free fingers and came to a letter from American Express. Surely their card was going to be canceled. A particularly expressive wordless cry came from his lips and Astrid tried for it all. He could feel the irony all the way to the center of his stomach. He stood as long as he could, then sank faintly into a chair.

After a moment, Astrid said, "What do you have in your hand?"

She pulled the crumpled letter from his grasp. Her brow darkened. "They're dropping us, huh?"

"Who?"

"Are you pretending you haven't seen this?"

Joe shook his head.

A peculiar look flickered across Astrid's face. "Has this been a great blow to you?" she asked.

"I can't win," said Joe. The thing was, he loved Astrid. And he could have brought out better things in her than he had. He brought out things in Astrid that were bad and went around disliking her for them. He sat in his chair and mused about his own unfairness as the wind pressed green masses of Florida holly to the window. "My character," he said, "is composed almost strictly of things I hate in other people."

They were under a new pressure. They were going to have to live on less because of Joe's difficulty with his work and the sudden termination of the lease money. None of the explanations Joe received from his Aunt Lureen made sense or persuaded him. He was suspicious that his Uncle Smitty was somehow getting the money from his sister. At first, he'd felt that if it meant enough to them to just take it, they could go ahead and do so. Though it was a technicality, the ranch was in Lureen's name and, as a technical thing, she could do as she pleased. But that was not the understanding she had with Joe's father, blood to blood, and she knew it. On this note, Joe could get indignant. Sometimes it passed. Sometimes it embarrassed him and sometimes the whole thing made him feel guilty. The worst part of it was that Ivan would come to sense that Joe had less choice about whether or not to do his projects. Ivan said it pained him to see an old friend refuse to abandon himself to the fiesta of consumption that was our national life.

Astrid came over and sat next to him. "Don't be so hard on yourself," she said.

"I always promised myself that in the future I would quit living in the future. But I may have to do a little planning now."

"Joe," she said, "why don't you call some friends? I'm going out. I'm tired of this. Or at least, I'm not interested in this. It's time to do something."

Joe made a few calls to people he knew out West. About the time he got off the phone, Astrid was back carrying packages. She set them down, picked up the hall rug, and gave it a pop. She popped the rug as if she was in a bullfight. Joe's mood had sunk even further since he'd been calling around Montana.

The next time Ivan came down from New York, he took them out to dinner. By the time they got to the restaurant, which was situated next to the ocean on its own band of seagrape-shaded beach, the sun had gone down and the sunset watchers had finished their drinks and were heading home for dinner. Astrid wore her hair up, pinned with a rose-colored enamel flower. Joe accompanied her with his hand lightly rested in the pleasant curve in the small of her back. Ivan Slater seemed to be rushing, though he walked no faster than they did. "I hope I'm not late," he said. "I got caught up watching TV, Oprah Winfrey squeezing the shit out of some little white lady." He wore a blousy Cuban shirt and had rolled his pants up in some ghastly sartorial reference to peasantry; instead of appropriate sandals or huaraches, he wore the lace-up black street shoes of his more accustomed venues in New York. Nevertheless, he bounded along confidently without actually going faster than his companions. He was marketing a thing called "The Old Vermont Dog Mill," which was a treadmill exerciser for overweight suburban labradors that also served to grind coffee and provide the power for a kitchen knife sharpener. It seemed impossible that he didn't see the ridiculousness of this but he didn't; he saw only opportunity. When Joe thought of the developing problems with the grazing lease and imagined he could be reduced to working with Ivan on the Old Vermont Dog Mill, he was chilled deep within.

They got a table on the deck under the seagrapes and immediately began to look into their menus as though they had a job to get through.

"That's not good conch salad," said Joe. "It's chum."

"Don't start in," said Astrid.

"Are stone crabs in season?" asked Ivan.

"Who knows," said Joe. "I don't know."

"The tone is burn-out plus," said Astrid.

"Ivan," said Joe, "why don't you get your own girlfriend? The waiter thinks this is a ménage à trois. Ditto the maitre d'."

"You've asked this same question since our school days."

"Never getting an answer."

"I do have girlfriends but they are never presentable."

"You could present them to us," said Astrid. "We would be prepared to understand almost anything."

"You talk brave," said Ivan.

"We could take them if they were truly awful," Astrid said. "It's the little things that suck."

When their dinners came, there seemed to be almost nothing on the plate. Joe understood that this was in response to current views on cuisine held in France; and of course that helped to justify the price, but Joe was hungry. He tapped the tines of his fork all around the empty areas of his plate as though probing for food. Astrid was annoyed with him and gave him furious looks, and the waiter sighed operatically.

"If you were back in Montana," she said, "undoubtedly they would put a great haunch before you and you would be happier."

"That's right."

There was a whirlwind of activity as Ivan began to eat.

"Joe," said Astrid, "I've been here all my life and you are a classic snowbird. After basking in the sun for a couple of years, you got ironic about everything."

"He's homesick," said Ivan through his food. "When you're homesick and home is three thousand miles away and you're broke and there's a gulf of communication between you and the faggot waiter and the plate is half empty before you half start, your heart is sore afflicted."

"Thank you, Ivan," said Joe.

"You like a quality of care and selection in your life, Joe. I like life bulging at the seams," Ivan said.

"I like it with loud music and hot sauce," said Astrid.

"Because you're Cuban," Joe said.

"That's racist, actually," Astrid said.

"I'm serious, Joe," Ivan said. "Don't be so meticulous. Quit weighing things out. It's neurotic. Man was made to consume. Say yes to fucking well everything."

The waiter looked significantly at Astrid. They were friends. In three years, Joe had not gotten used to Astrid's friends. The waiter accepted the little illness of her hanging around with straight men. A bright wave caught the lights of the restaurant and rolled obliquely onto the beach. The restaurant was beginning to fill. Joe felt the smile on his face fade pleasantly. Astrid put a cigarette in her mouth and waited for Ivan to light it. Joe enjoyed their friendship. He loved the sight of Astrid smoking, while angry people at neighboring tables waved into the air around them.

Astrid's uncompliant nature made her the only woman friend of Ivan's life. Joe watched with approval. Sexless friendships reminded him of children. Quite lovely until someone whipped it out.

So once again Joe and Ivan were going to work together. Ivan was inspired by this work he was doing; Joe was trying to accept its necessity. At one time he had painted and had some acceptance; but he painted so slowly at the best of times and was so seldom sufficiently moved by an idea that he had to

HAILEY PUBLIC LIBRARY

take work that did not depend upon strong feelings. Lately, he wasn't really painting at all. He was trying to "face it," a phrase Astrid found overpoweringly bleak. He told her he had sold out; she said he lacked sufficient mental health to sell out. "I'm going to face it," he said.

"Don't face it, for Christ's sake," she said.

Now Joe watched gloomily as Ivan paid the bill. When the waiter went off with his credit card, Ivan asked, "What's twenty percent of ninety-three dollars?"

Joe groaned.

"Crass!" called Astrid.

Out in front, intensity was building. The hostess had gold-rimmed glasses hanging on her bosom from a chain. She only put them on to check dubious reservations in the big book on the stand. There was a line and Joe was pleased they had eaten early. They walked onto the street where the suave shapes of automobiles, parked on the fallen palm fronds, glowed in the streetlights. The breaking surf could be heard and Joe admitted to himself the tremendous romance this seemed to imply, though it always seemed to remain in the world of implication. He felt like an old steer with its head under the fence straining for that grass just over there.

They got into Ivan's rental car. Ivan did not start it up immediately. The streetlight shining through the coconut palms lit up all six of their knees. "Joe," Ivan said, "you're very quiet. And I know you, Joe. You are my friend since we stood shoulder to shoulder in the school lavatory popping zits, betting our pride on the hope of hitting the mirror. But this quiet, this looking off, is a calm before the storm, which I know and have seen before, Joe. I only ask that you remember a few commitments and that you be a gentleman about it, if it kills you. I say all this knowing it may be well out of reach for you."

Ivan looked straight ahead through the windshield. Joe looked straight ahead through the windshield. Astrid looked at Joe.

Joe said, "Start it up."

8

In offering Joe the use of her car the next morning, a small pink convertible, Astrid had naively said to get a pound of snapper fillets and a choice of two vegetables and Joe had said he'd be back in a minute. Now clouds settled in the upper curve of the windshield, slowly wiped around, and disappeared. The yellow center line ticked in the side mirror. Lizards and tropical foliage managed to survive in the atmosphere of a New York subway. The traffic on the great divided parkway moved at a trancelike evenness maintained by the Florida Highway Patrol. He wanted to keep moving in case Astrid reported her car stolen.

In the end it was a day that was missing from Joe's life. He didn't turn on the radio until he left his motel near Pensacola the next morning. He realized he was about to hit the real torso of America and his spirits rose. He crossed into Alabama and took a few minutes out to view an arts and crafts fair in a vast baking parking lot. It was as if a thousand garages had been emptied onto a runway. Solemn people stood behind tables that held wan attempts at art in oil and ceramics and a twentieth-century history of appliances. Portraits of Elvis on black velvet. He pulled out onto the highway and resumed, having to go very slow for a mile until he could pass a pickup truck full of yellow lawn chairs. Battered, rusted cars passed with hard faces framed by Beatles-type haircuts. It seemed that before he even reached the Mississippi line, the sky had begun to grow, to widen: at the Escatawpa River the pines strained upward against a terrific expanse of blue sky. The highway was empty. The clouds stretching down to the horizon majestically ruled the scene. Joe was filled with a mad sense of freedom, free to eat fast food, free to sleep with a stranger. Instead of solving his problems, he had become someone without problems, a kind of ghost.

He passed a little bayou where a young fellow in knee-length surfer shorts covered with beer commercials watched a bobber rest on the mirror surface of water. This plain scene held a great mystery for him. There was a lovely waterland around the Pascagoula River with silver curves showing through the sea grass for a great distance while the road crossed in low, loping arcs. He stopped and watched fishermen unloading crab boats. He walked down and sat on a broken-off piling. A woman handed an old fisherman a pint of whiskey in a paper bag. She said, "If you beat me up like you did last weekend, I ain't going to buy you no more of that." Joe heard this with amazement.

He went to sleep in a motel. Outside in the parking lot, a couple leaned up against their car and listened to James Cotton sing the blues. "I don't like white and white don't like me." Joe thought about that as he lay in bed. He couldn't quite understand why, lying in this unknown motel in this unknown place, he felt such a desperate joy.

.

At seven in the morning, he was rolling through Danville Parish, Louisiana. Pine forests stood on the high ground between the bayous, pine pollen filling the air so that the car was covered with pollen and the air was so heavy with pollen there were times he thought he ought to turn on the headlights to see. But rush hour in Shreveport was different from other rush hours, the thickness of humidity, the crazy songs on the radio, flirtation between speeding automobiles. Secession had worked! The marquee in front of the Louisiana State Fairground announced county pig champions and English rock and roll bands. The radio advertised bass boats, fire ant control potions and the Boot Hill Racetrack.

Joe thought that crossing into Texas and getting past the Red River would give him the feeling of being back out West but it didn't happen. The thunderstorms lashed the highway and it still looked like Louisiana with all the gums and hickories and tupelos. A home repair truck passed with a sign on its side that said, "Obsessed to serve the customer." Nothing halfway about the South. Someone shot up behind Joe in a little Japanese car, face pressed against the windshield, passed, then lost his motivation. Roostertailing through the rainwater, Joe had to pass him again. The cloudburst intensified and a mile or two down the road toward Longview, Texas, a pickup truck went into sideways slow motion, slid across the meridian and went into the ditch. Three men got out and stared at it. These men seemed to feel their pickup owed them an explanation. Once he reached Longview, he could see back to the thunderstorm, see its grand and sculptural shape, its violent black underside. The radio said they were glad about the rain because it would keep the pollen down and people could get some relief from their allergies and wasn't that what people wanted, some relief? Joe liked it for the feeling of dropping a curtain between him and the past, a welcome curtain. This was the highway and he was a ghost. It was a relief.

Somewhere past the Sabine River, Joe started to spot the little oil patches, the active ones with bright painted pumps, bobbing away and pumping oil. And oil patches that had seen better days, with their pumps stopped and the paint rusted off like a field full of giant grasshoppers that had died or reached some eerie state beyond normal death. The radio had used the phrase "nuclear winter" and increasingly Joe was relying on the radio to shape his thoughts. He was still thinking about fire ants. Fire ants in the nuclear winter.

Van Zandt, Texas, was blushing green in a deeply wooded succession of gentle, rolling woodlands. For thirty-five seconds, Joe ached to live there. Then by Terrell, glad to no longer live in Van Zandt, he was out of the woodlands and in an ugly cattle country that looked like Iowa where there were no fire ants and pollen and mulattoes in convertibles, and no race music on the radio. Joe went blank and stayed that way until he came over a big long ascent and there below him was a cloud of mesquite and telegraph wires and glittering buildings. The hard angles of light on each surface seemed to communicate that the West had begun and he was on his way home. The sky picked up the white edges of the ravines, rocks and subdivisions equally. The skyscrapers cheerfully said, "We see you passing, you ghost! So long, Joe-Buddy!" This was Dallas!

There was a perfect Texan urban river bottom at Grand Prairie with scrub willows whose roots gathered trash in the flash floods that shot through new neighborhoods. Joe was maddened by joy at being in the country of the West. He felt that he would find a restored coordination for his life here. This was the West's job. Gustav Mahler of all people was on the radio. Great Southwest Parkway! Lone Star Homes! Texas Toyota! A subdivision of multifarious grandeur, half-timbered Tudor homes baking in the dry air and clinging to the hillsides. A sign in front read *From the 80's.* Joe could not understand the message because he thought they were talking about the decade of these homes; then he realized they meant the price of the units. Holy fire ants! Little places like that?

He crossed the Trinity River in a bright sun that made approaching traffic flash its windshields in a stream of glitter, along the edge of the Fort Worth stockyards. A radio preacher shouted, "Satan is playing hardball!"

On an awful-looking scrapped-off former mesquite flat north of Fort Worth, he passed "Fossil Creek, The Community on the Green. Next right, Blue Mound, Texas." Getting on toward Wichita Falls, the radio briefly stilled, there began to be well-kept ranches, lots of horses, the houses on elevations with windmills to catch the breeze and fanciful entryways welded together out of rod and angle iron. Fetishistic paved driveways. There were things here in Texas that made Joe nervous, but he blamed it on whatever produced that radio religion, fire and brimstone delivered at a nice dance tempo.

It began to grow stormy looking and the conflict of spring and winter produced a cascading immensity of light that Joe felt levitate him as he drove in and out of vast shadows. State Highway Department trucks were ignited from within by a tremendous yellow light. The signs shone fiercely at him with their brusque messages. Railroad track crews were lit up like the cast of a Broadway show. A windy squall separated itself from the general pattern and arose before him like a dead king in an opera. A battered farm truck passed with a tuxedo hanging in the rear window. There were flattened armadillos on the road. The weather looked worrisome — worrisome and bad enough to drive him back to Astrid. Or, if it wasn't for the awkwardness of driving her car, he could have given her a call. He could have said, "I'm en route!"

So, he stopped at Henrietta and ate pinto beans and corn bread and listened to a distant kitchen radio issue fairly dire weather forecasts. The restaurant had wooden booths and a few young men in work clothes sat sideways in them with their arms over the back and spoke in courtly tones to the black-haired, aging waitress.

Back on the road, Joe saw at a considerable distance the British flag emblazoned on a solitary billboard. But when he drew close, it turned out to be an ad for Beech-Nut chewing tobacco. Tumbleweed blew furiously across the road near an old brick high school that stood like a depressing fortress against the distant horizon and slate, moving clouds. There were cotton fields and, here and there, cotton wagons were drawn up on the side roads. The sign in Quanah said, "Stop and Eat with Us. Willie Nelson Did." Joe noted that the goofy faces of the Deep South, the tragic and comic masks donned down there, had been replaced by a kind of belligerent stare. The highway signs said, "Don't Mess with Texas." It didn't look too damn friendly out there. Maybe it was the weather.

Right after he crossed the Prairie Dog Town Fork of the Red River a train approached from a distance. When it came close, all that was visible was its windshield; the rest was a vast blowing mound of snow and ice. What's going on here? Turn on the radio, my friend. He got another preacher, this one explaining that the mind does not work the exact-same as a Disposall and we cannot grind up the filth that goes into it. We must be careful not to put filth into it in the first place.

Suddenly, he was driving on a solid corrugation of ice in a

whiteout. It just dropped from the heavens and put an end to visibility. He hunched over the wheel as though to examine the road even more closely than he could in a normal seated position. The outer world was filled with phantom vehicles, some floating by at eye level, others sunk to one side plainly disabled. A human silhouette arose and vanished. It was terrifying. It was a regular bad dream. He thought, I am being punished for stealing, for doubting the truthfulness of my aunt and uncle in withholding my lease money, for not painting and for walking out on a good woman.

He came up behind a twenty-year-old luxury sedan heaving along sedately. He clove to that sedan. It had a bumper sticker that said *XIT Ranch Reunion* and Joe tried to tag it as it appeared and disappeared in the snow. He passed an old tractor-trailer rig full of fenceposts and woven wire jackknifed in the ditch. Then he lost the sedan; it seemed to dematerialize in the whiteness and he was alone. He slowed to ten miles an hour and felt his insides labor against the white indefinite distance before him.

A fashion center for babies was advertising on the radio. They had a special for those hard-to-shop-for preemies. Including diapers for their little thumb-size bottoms. Then all of a sudden, a great miracle occurred, simultaneous with news of these glorious infants. The sun came out on a perfect world in the middle of which, surrounded by hysterical people, a Greyhound Vista-Cruiser lay on its side: red, white, and blue with tinted windows, in the ditch. Joe crept by in case he was needed, but the passengers were having their moment as they watched the driver set out orange cautionary cones, and they didn't seem to need or want Joe, who had not been with them when it happened but rather with the well-dressed babies of the radio.

A little way past the town of Goodnight, he could see cattle running the fenceline in wild amazement at nature. A truck went by like the home repair truck back in Louisiana but this one said, "Don't sleep with a drip—Call a plumber!" The day was almost done. Joe flew through the slush to Amarillo, took a room, ate in a Japanese restaurant and went to bed. He felt like he was breaking his back trying to get through Texas. This ghost wanted to go home.

The next day, before he was fully awake, before he had had any opportunity for banishing thoughts, he was in Cimarron County, Oklahoma, where the wind blew so hard the shadows flew on the roadway and where, stopping on the edge of a plowed field, he had to lean backward into the wind to take a leak and even then it just sprayed from his dick like sleet. The radio said that Kansas steer prices were down because several of the packing plants had been closed by blizzards. Joe drove on. Near the horizon, there was the most overcrowded feedlot of Black Angus cattle Joe had ever seen. He stared at it until he overtook what turned out to be a vast depot of worn-out automobile tires, extending over many acres.

He began to see mountains and his spirit rose with the accumulating altitude, kept climbing until it sank again around Monument Hill and new snow and population; finally he was in the Denver rush hour, which caused him to sink into complete apathy as he took his place in the teeming lanes.

He cleared out of north Denver, traffic thinning about the

time he passed a vast illuminated dog track, amazing against the darkening Front Range. It was dark and wild and cold after that, after the St. Vrain River and the Wyoming line. A genuine ground blizzard was falling by the time he got to Cheyenne, so he stopped at a place called Little America, the home of fifty-five gas pumps, and slept like a baby, knowing all that gasoline was out there. There was enough gasoline for a homesick person to drive home millions of times. Joe was hugely annoyed to have had this thought.

He was gone before daybreak, following a Haliburton drilling equipment truck with a sign on its rear that said it braked for jackalope. Joe's sense of mission had reached a burning pitch and he tailgated the big rig over sections of road varnished by the manure that ran out of the cattle trucks. The two vehicles went down through Wyoming in a treacherous eighty mile an hour syncopation.

Wheatland, Wyoming, had sentimental Spanish haciendas out in the windswept tank farm at the edge of the sage. A somber and detached-looking herd of buffalo stared out at the highway across five strands of barbed wire. Tonight was going to be Olde Southe Gumbo Night at the restaurant in Douglas where Joe released the Haliburton truck and stopped for breakfast. There was an array of condiments that suggested people ate at all hours here. Joe examined the salad dressing. It looked like the styling gel in a beauty parlor. Buddy Holly sang "True Love Waits" from a red and chrome speaker at the end of his booth. While he ate, the sun burst out like a hostile and metallic stunt. Beyond the window, the land of the jackalope shone under a burnishing wind.

Back on the highway, a sheriff's car shot past with a little gray-haired prisoner in the back. Joe drove until he reached Kaycee, not much more than a small depression in the ground east of the highway: gas station, quonset buildings, a few houses. He stopped and bought some homemade elk sausage from a man he knew there. He was getting close.

The Tongue River was green and low and clear. It was the last thing he noticed until he crossed into Montana. At Crow Agency a sign said, "Jesus Is Lord on the Crow Reservation." Loose horses were also Lord on the Crow reservation. An ambulance tore off down a dirt road, its red light throbbing like a severed artery.

Three hours later he drove through his old hometown, Deadrock. He took a left by the switching yard and took the dirt road south toward the ranch. He followed the river bottom back to his house. Before long, the cottonwoods would make a cloudy tunnel for the racing stream but they were just now beginning to leaf out; and where the stream broadened out and flowed in flat pastures, its every turn was marked by an even growth of willows. The light flashed on the shallow streams that fed the river where they emerged from their grassy tunnels; and in the marshy stands of cattail, blackbirds jumped up and showered down once again. A rancher went alongside the road, a great fat man on a small motorcycle. He had his shovel and fabric dams lashed behind him and his felt hat pulled down so firmly against the wind that it bowed his ears out. A small collie lay across his lap as he sputtered along. Some of the fields had great splashes of pasture ruining yellow spurge. The ditch bank along the road was a garden of early spring wild flowers, shooting stars, forget-me-nots, lupine. Snow still lay collected in the shade. You couldn't really tell you had left one ranch and gone onto another. A cattle guard marked the actual boundary but the rolling country was the same in every direction. The house sat down in some trees, old trees that were splotched with dead branches. There was a seasonal creek underneath the trees but it had dried up now into nothing but a wash. A half-acre had been fenced to enclose the place but the cattle had beaten the ground down right to the boundaries.

The door was unlocked. Joe went in and looked around. There wasn't much for furnishings but there was enough. There was a woodstove, an old Frigidaire, and two army blankets on the bunk. The toilet bowl was stained with iron but it worked. Someone had fixed the well. There was a table in the kitchen. And the phone worked. Not owning or even caring about any of it made this seem blissful. His nights wouldn't be interrupted by bad dreams. It was going to be all right.

10

When Joe's father began leasing the pasture to the Overstreets, the ranch began to go downhill. The house started toward its present moldering state; the fences were kept in what minimal condition would hold cattle but where the property adjoined the lessors, the fences were allowed to fall and be walked into the ground by herds of cows. The pastures were eaten down year after year until the buck brush, wild currants and sage had begun to advance across their surfaces, with the result that the carrying capacity dropped and with it, the grazing fees. Evaporation from the stripped ground reduced the discharge of the good springs to trickles; the marginal springs had long since been milled to mud by cattle and finally the mud itself had dried up and sealed the springs. But the worst problems of the ranch existed at the level of paper, where liens and assumptions clouded its title.

At first, it hadn't mattered. Joe had had a good enough career painting; he had found handy equivalents with Ivan Slater and others, all somewhat in anticipation of his desire to resume his work.

Joe had sometimes felt that it would be a great relief to give up on recovering his talent; and now he was facing, in the confines of approaching maturity, the fact that he was broke and there was nothing new, nothing at the edge of things, nothing around the corner that would save him. He hoped he wouldn't soon be known as the man who evicted his own kinfolk from their ancestral pasturage.

Joe had come to believe from reading books that in many landholding families, there existed perfect communication between the generations about the land itself. He noticed how many Southerners believed this. Even if they were in New York there was always a warmhearted old daddy holding out for their possession and occupancy an ancient farm — viewed as a sacred tenure on earth rather than agriculture — whenever they should choose to take it up. Price of admission? Take a few minutes, after the soul-stirring train ride down yonder, to make friends with the resident darkies. Where had people gone wrong in the West? In the latest joke, leaving a ranch to one's children was called child abuse. But Joe couldn't really take that view. He had to go see Lureen and straighten things out.

It had gotten too quiet in the neighborhood. There used to be a roar of roller skates on the sidewalk. The small garage next to the house was empty. It had once held his Uncle Smitty's Ford, a car he called his "foreign car." "It's foreign to me," Smitty explained. Many years ago, Smitty came home from the war. He never left after that.

Joe walked around to the side entrance of the house, the only one anyone had ever used. The front door opened onto a hallway and then into a large sitting room that was reserved for the high ceremonies of the day. He remembered how the furniture was kept covered, dreadful shapes, the drapes drawn until life could resume on a special occasion. Children, who were allowed every liberty in the other rooms, including the right to bay down the laundry chute, build matchstick rockets, and even play in the avalanche of coal in the cellar, were frightened in this room. Joe's grandmother sat for weeks here after her husband died as though the dream of respectability they had shared was alive in its sad furnishings, its curio cabinet, its damask-covered love seat and its solitary volume of Elizabeth Barrett Browning. When the silence of his grandmother's mourning overpowered the rest of the family, Joe was sent to see her. She sat with her hands in her lap and her feet crossed under her chair. He moved to her side and she didn't respond. He knew he had to say something but he could smell new rain on the sidewalk and know that already things were going on that consigned his grandfather to the past. His mind moved to that miracle. "I was wondering," he mused, in his little-old-man style, "if Grandpa happened to leave me any gold." Joe's grandmother stared, and began to laugh. She laughed for minutes while he examined the postcards, fossils and pressed flowers in the curio cabinet, ignoring her laugh and thinking about the curiosities and the miracle of rain, of opportunities beyond the funereal door. There was a ring of keys fused together by fire that he held in awe. His grandmother got up and looked around as though recovering from a spell. She walked straight back into her life, revitalized by the cold musing of a child.

Joe knocked. In a moment the door opened and there stood his Aunt Lureen in a blue flowered dress and white coat sweater. She held her face, compressed her cheeks, and cried, "He's back!" A cloud crossed her face. The sight of Joe seemed to produce a hundred contradictory thoughts.

"Yes," Joe said. "I'm back, all right!" For some reason, he whistled. A maladroit quality of enthusiasm seemed to penetrate the air and the sharp whistling brought it up to pitch.

Joe hugged Lureen — she was small and strong — and followed her self-effacing step into the house with its wooden smells, its smells of generations of work clothes and vagaries of weather, of sporting uniforms and overcoats, straight into the vast kitchen which more than anything recalled the thriving days when they had watched game shows from behind TV trays. Joe's oldest memory was of his Uncle Smitty standing up in his army uniform and announcing, "I for one am proud to be an American." Joe had a photograph of Smitty from his army days, a hard young face that seemed to belong to the '40s, the collar of his officer's tunic sunk into his neck, Joe's grandparents beaming at him. There was nothing in that picture to hint that little would go right for Smitty.

Aunt Lureen carried the tea tray into the dining room. You could see the drop of the street to the trestle for a train that used to cancel talk in its roaring traverse. She had never married, never even had a beau. She had radiated duty from the beginning, a duty which lay basically elsewhere, a broad, sexless commitment to vagary, that is, to others.

"Weren't you an angel to come see us," said Lureen, staring with admiration. Joe poured the tea, thinking, That's just a pleasant formality and of course there is no need for me to reply specifically. Around them the halls and rooms seemed to express a detailed emptiness. "What have you been doing, Joe?" The words of these questions fell like stones dropped into a deep well. Joe thought if he could just get some conversational rhythm going, this wouldn't be such a strain. He had long since lost his nerve to ask about the lease.

"I've been on the road. That's about all I've got to say for myself."

"Doing what?"

"Little deal going there with the space program." What a childish lie! The space program was all he could think of about Florida. That and coconuts. If he had been doing anything there, he wouldn't be here. He had struck a void but he could scarcely tell her he no longer knew what he was doing.

"How did you enjoy working in the space program?"

"Well, I got out in one piece," said Joe. He thought this peculiar reference to himself in an atmosphere which included the explosion of a space shuttle would add solemnity to this occasion. In the world of coconuts, there would be no real parallel. But Lureen missed the gravity of his remark. She bent over in laughter. It was as if he had picked coconuts after all. How painful it was!

Everything was magnified. Lureen's chaste little paintings were on the wall. It had been her escape during decades of school teaching; the bouquets, the curled-up kittens, the worn-out slippers next to the pipe and pouch, the waterfall, all made a kind of calendar of her days. Her pictures reflected her tidy view of a family life she hadn't had.

Smitty could be heard coming in through the kitchen, a lurching, arhythmic tread on the old wooden floor, whistling "Peg o' My Heart." Then he roared; but this was from afar, a great and bitterly insincere braying. His appearance was anticlimactic, his carefully combed auburn hair, his ironic face, his handsomely tailored but not so clean blue suit, making one wonder as he appeared in the parlor, who *did* roar in the next room, surely not this person whose face swam with in-decision. Smitty had spent many years now in what he called "study" and his shabby-genteel presence was entirely in-

vented. What had become of the hard-faced soldier of the
'40s?

"Joe, my God it's you."

"Home at last."

"A good tan, I see."

"Pretty hot."

"Your late lamented father could have used a trip or two to
the Sun Belt. He might have lived longer."

Joe didn't say anything in reply.

"But when you've pulled yourself up by your bootstraps,
palm trees seem to be thin stuff. Will you join me for a drink?"

"Not right now. Lureen and I are having a visit."

"Ah," said Smitty. "Then this must be my stop."

Smitty suggested by sheer choreography that an appoint-
ment awaited him. When he'd gone, Joe said, "Smitty hasn't
changed."

"No, we can count on Smitty."

"Has he gone out for a drink?"

"It won't amount to much. No money."

"Well, that's good," said Joe, making the remark as minimal
as possible. A quick look of annoyance crossed Lureen's face.
There was something here Joe couldn't quite follow. He felt
like a parasite. He might as well have said, "Smitty is drinking
the lease."

Lureen said, "We've done the best we could."

Smitty stuck his red face in the doorway. "Joe, may I see
you a moment?" The face hung there until it was confirmed
Joe would come.

Joe got up and followed him into the parlor. There was a
small desk with a leather panel in its top and a chair behind
it. Smitty pulled an armchair up for Joe and seated himself
opposite, at the desk. He was agitated as he drew some old

forms out of the drawer and placed them on the desk top. Joe could hear children bouncing a rubber ball off the side of the house. Lureen would attend to them shortly. She viewed children as other people view horseflies. Her gentleness disappeared in their presence. They feared her instinctively. Joe heard the shout and the ball bouncing stopped.

"Joe," Smitty said, "I'm right in the middle of a deal that will produce my fortune. We make our own luck, don't you agree? It's funny that after years in the insurance business I should have come up with this! But to my own astonishment I find myself getting into seafood, which is all the rage in this diet-conscious time, shrimp to be exact, Gulf Coast shrimp which I am going to import into Montana! Et cetera, et cetera, but anyway, do you have life insurance?" Smitty clasped his hands on top of the papers in the manner of a concerned benefactor. "I know it's a far cry from shrimp!"

"No."

"Can you appreciate that I am an agent for American Mutual? That is, until that mountain of crustaceans begins rolling North!"

"No, actually, Uncle Smitty, I didn't know that."

"Well, I am. And while I disapprove of nepotism, the smoke-filled room and scratching one another's backs, I am in a position to enhance the advantages you already possess by virtue of your youth." He began to write on one of the forms. "I think I can spell your name," he chuckled. "Don't worry, lad! You're not buying life insurance! And I can find out from Lureen what you're using for an address these days!" Joe began to relax again. "This is just a request to quote you some rates, which will be mailed to your home, sometime . . . hence." He folded up the papers decisively and placed them back in the drawer.

"Thank you," said Joe in a wave of relief.

"You, sir, are welcome."

"I look forward to going over those rates."

"At your leisure, at your leisure. I'm certainly in no rush, what with an avalanche of pink headed my way from the Texas coast!"

Joe clapped his hands on his knees preparatory to rising. "Shall we?"

"One small matter," Smitty said. Joe froze. "The rather small matter, of the filing fee."

Joe slapped at his pants pockets. "I'm not sure I—"

"Have your wallet? I can help there. You do have it. And the filing fee, which is nominal by any civilized standards and which does not begin to recompense me for the time I will have to put in, comes to twenty dollars."

Joe got his wallet out. He peered at the bills like a timid card player.

"There's one!" said Smitty, plucking a twenty into midair. He was immediately on his feet, an expression not of triumph but of horrible relief on his face. "With any luck, and assuming you pass the physical, you will be able to direct a windfall to an heir of your choice. In your generation, where the act of procreation has been reduced to a carnival, you might have your hands full picking a favorite! And now I excuse myself." He shot out the door.

When Joe returned to his aunt, she said, "Did you give him any money?"

"I'm afraid I did."

"Well," she said, "I'm sure he needed it for something important."

It was a formality with Lureen, when short of other topics or in any way embarrassed, to deplore Montana's failing industries. She started in today on the collapse of the cattle industry, the ill effects of the Texas and Midwestern feedlots, the evils of hedging and the betrayal of the agricultural family unit by Secretary of Agriculture Earl Butz. She attacked the usurious practices of the Burlington Northern Railroad, the victimization of the Golden Triangle wheat man and the sabotage of the unions by neo-fascist strawmen posing as shop stewards. It took her out of herself, out of her meekness; and it made Joe extraordinarily uncomfortable to watch her form a timid oratory behind this array of facts. When she was through, she folded her hands like a child who has just finished playing a piece on the piano.

Joe tried to look out the window, anywhere.

"Joe, right after you got back, Mr. Overstreet announced that he was dropping his lease with us," Lureen said.

"I wondered where it went. My check hasn't come in a long time."

"Even before that, we, Smitty and I, had got into some, uh, some projects. Which we expect will do just fine. I don't know what came over Mr. Overstreet. We've had that arrangement for *so* long."

"Well, who else can you get?"

"I really don't know. Overstreets have us surrounded. I really don't know who else would want it. It's kind of unhandy. And the grass is good this year. I'd even buy the yearlings if someone would run them for me." Joe was paralyzed by sudden excitement.

"You mean, you'd need someone to just run the place for a while?" Joe asked.

"Now that Overstreets have let it go, I really don't know anyone out there I could ask. Do you have any ideas?"

"I'll do it!" Joe said. "Let me do that."

"Would you really?"

Smitty banged through the kitchen and entered the room once again but with an air of tremendous renewal. Joe was frustrated. Smitty had donned what seemed to Joe to be a fairly astounding outfit: two-tone leather evening slippers and a jacket of English cut, a kind of round-shouldered smoking jacket in pearl gray wool, tied with a royal red sash. He had a drink in his hand and a large book, which he reached over to Joe. He sat down in a Windsor chair next to Lureen, lacing his fingers around the drink and resting his chin on his chest while his eyes burned in Joe's direction. In this cheap house, in a modest town, he had achieved a tone of specious artifice usually available only to the very successful. Joe felt the excitement, the need to be wary.

"This is a book," Smitty intoned, then seemed to lose his train of thought. "This, sir, is a book," he began again.

"I see that it is," Joe said.

Smitty delivered a weary sigh, Lord Smitty peering from a dizzying aerie.

"It is Roget's"—what satisfaction it seemed to give him to intone the two voluptuous vowels of "Roget's"!—"*Thesaurus.*" This last was said with such abrupt concussion it was like a sneeze. "And it is a gift from me . . . to you."

"Thank you," said Joe.

"Here is how Roget's Thesaurus is to be employed. First look up the key words you wish to use. They will all be big ones. But this book will tell you the *little plain words* that *little plain people* like your aunt and I know and in this way you will be able to make yourself understood to us. Neither of us is in the space program."

"I expect it will come in very handy," said Joe. He reached out and accepted the book from Smitty's hands. Smitty gazed

71

at him with what looked like all the world to be hatred, then made another of his formal departures, raising a forefinger to level one of Lureen's watercolors.

"I wonder what brought that on," said Joe. A sharp tinkling sound was heard repeatedly from the direction of the kitchen, almost the sound of Christmas decorations falling from the tree. Joe looked at his aunt; she looked back. They headed for the kitchen. There they found Smitty with a tray poised over one shoulder like a waiter. It held a quantity of crystal stemware that had belonged to Joe's mother. With his free hand Smitty took up each glass by its base and hurled it to the floor, where it burst. His auburn hair was flung out in every direction and it reminded Joe of some old picture of the devil.

With a pixieish expression, Smitty's gaze moved from Joe to Lureen and then back. He held a glass by its stem. He paused. He turned his eyes to the glass. In slow motion, the glass inverted and began its descent to the floor. Joe watched. It seemed to take a very long time and then it became a silver star to the memory of Joe's mother. It disappeared in the debris of its predecessors. Smitty sent the remainder of the glasses to the floor with a motion like a shot-putter, even tipping up on one slippered toe. Then he relaxed. Nothing had happened really, had it? All for the best, somehow. Still, thought Joe, it makes for a rather long evening.

"Why don't I show you your room," said Lureen, "and we can get caught up on our rest." Because it had become ridiculous to let this pass without remark, she lowered her voice to say that "everyone," meaning Smitty, had problems which Joe couldn't be expected to understand because he hadn't been around. Smitty stood right there and listened blithely.

"Taking this all in?" Joe asked Smitty quietly.

"Mm-hm."

"You know," Lureen mused desperately, "Duffy's Fourth of July at Flathead Lake was a hundred years ago." Joe had no idea what to do with that one other than take it as an obscure family reference intended to restore the intimacy she had withdrawn. Duffy's Fourth of July at Flathead Lake. What was that?

"Joe doesn't know what you're talking about," sang Smitty. Then he turned to Joe. "You are among friends," he said gravely. "Think of it: your own flesh and blood." He leaned his weight in the pockets of his robe like an old trainer watching his racehorses at daybreak. All his gestures seemed similarly detached from his surroundings. Smitty walked up to the barometer and gave the glass a tap. This seemed to give him his next idea. "I think I'll head for my quarters now," he said. "The artillery has begun to subside. Another day tomorrow. One more colorful than the other."

When Smitty left the room, humming "The Caissons Go Rolling Along," a queer tension set in. Joe knew now his arrival was an invasion, his presence abusive. He thought of making up alarming lies about the space program, ones he could deliver tearfully, accounts of loyal Americans shredded by titanium and lasers. If some sort of guilt based on an unimpeachable national purpose could be held over Lureen, possibly this miserable tone could be altered. "I delivered the little things to the space shuttle that made it a home, the nail clippers, the moisturizers, the paperbacks, the tampons . . ."

But the tension didn't last. He went back into the kitchen and helped her clean up the broken glass. Lureen held the dustpan. Joe tried to sweep carefully without letting the straws of the broom spring and scatter bits of crystal. He wanted to ask Lureen why she stood for it, but he didn't. They swept all around the great gas stove. As Joe knelt to hold the dustpan, he saw that its pipes had been disconnected. It was a dummy, a front for the mean little microwave next to the toaster.

"A service for twenty," Lureen said, referring to the broken crystal. "Who in this day and age needs a service for twenty?" A laugh of astonishment. Who indeed! My mother needed it, Joe thought. From each window of the kitchen, each except the one that opened on the tiny yard, could be seen the clapboard walls of the neighboring houses, the shadows of clotheslines just out of sight above, duplexes that used to be family homes. A service for twenty! They laughed desperately. How totally out of date! And finally, how removed from the space program! I don't feel so good, he thought.

"Joe, Smitty and I have made not such a bad life for ourselves here," Lureen said after they finished cleaning up. "We never have gotten used to the winters. And you know what we talk about? Hawaii. It's funny how those things start. Arthur Godfrey used to have a broadcast from Honolulu. He had a Hawaiian gal named Holly Loki on the show. Smitty and I used to listen. We kind of formed a picture. Someday, we thought . . . Hawaii! Well, Joe, let's really do call it a day." Lureen led him up the narrow wood stairs to the second floor. Joe tried to think of surf, a ukulele calling to him from the night-shrouded side of a sacred volcano, of outrigger canoes. He tried to put Smitty and Lureen in this scene and he just couldn't. Nothing could uproot them from their unhappy home. Not even a no-holds-barred luau.

Joe's old room looked onto a narrow rolling street. Lureen wanted him to spend the night before going back to the ranch in the morning. You could make out the railroad bridge and the big rapid river beyond. There was a stand next to his door with a pitcher of water on it. Joe's bed had been turned back. The room was sparely furnished with a small desk where Lureen stored her things: paper clips, Chapsticks, pencils. Joe pulled open the drawer as he'd loved to do thirty years before to smell the camphor from the Chapsticks. The pencils were in hard yellow bundles, the paper clips in small green cardboard boxes. The train went over the bridge like a comet, the little faces in the lighted windows racing through their lives. Joe's father had been raised here; his uncles had gone to two world wars from here; educations and paper routes and bar examinations had been prepared for in the kitchen here. Everyone rushing for the end like the people on the train. Smitty came home from the war after a booby trap had killed his best friend and stayed drunk for two years in the very room he occupied now. Joe's father used to say, "I went over too." And Smitty would say, "You didn't go over where I went over."

"Good night," said Lureen. Family business had worn her out. Instead of acknowledging her exhaustion, she had nominated Hawaii, whose blue-green seas would wash her all clean.

"Good night, Aunt Lureen," Joe sang out with love.

Joe stretched out in the dark, under the covers of the squeaking iron bed. He had slept here off and on his whole life. But now he felt like someone trying to hold a tarp down in the wind. He smoked in the dark. It was perfect. Smoking meant so much more now that he knew what it did to him. But in the dark it was perfect. He could see the cloud of his smoke rise like a ghost.

He must have fallen asleep because when he heard Smitty's voice, it was its emphasis that startled him; he had not heard what had gone on before. "For God's sake, Lureen, we're in a brownout! Keep the shade drawn."

Joe struck a match and looked at the dial of the loud clock ticking away beside him. It was after midnight. A husky laugh from Smitty rang through the upstairs, a man-of-action laugh. Joe had to have a look.

Lureen's room at the end of the hall was well lighted. Smitty and Lureen stood in its doorway like figures on a bandstand. Smitty wore his lieutenant's uniform and impatiently flipped his forage cap against his thigh. "We move at daybreak," he said.

"The bars closed an hour ago," said Lureen wearily.

"We pour right in behind the tanks and stay there until we get to Belgium," he insisted.

"Smitty," said Lureen, "I heard the radio! Truman said it's over!"

Smitty scrutinized his sister's features. "Can you trust a man who never earned the job? Harry The Haberdasher never-earned-the-job."

"You can trust the radio!" Lureen cried. Smitty stared back.

"I should have listened, Lureen. I should have listened to you. The nation has probably taken to the streets. Am I still welcome?" Their figures wavered in the sprawling light.

"The most welcome thing in the world," said Lureen in a voice that astonished Joe with its feeling. Smitty gave her a hug. Joe watched and tried to understand and was choked by the beauty of their embrace. He wondered why he was so moved by something he couldn't understand.

11

This sale yard was a place ranchers took batches of cattle too small to haul to the public yard in Billings. You didn't go here in a cattle truck; you went in the short-range stock truck in all the clothes you owned because the cab heater went out ten years ago. Some went pulling a gooseneck trailer behind the pickup. You could unload either at one of the elevated chutes or at the ground-level Powder River Gate, which opened straight into a holding pen where the yard men, usually older ranchers who had gone broke or were semire-tired, sorted and classed the cattle for that day's sale. Joe stopped and looked back out into the pens to get an idea of the flow of cattle. It looked pretty thin and there was a cold rain blowing over everything. The yard men leaned on their long prods and stared out across the pens into nowhere.

Joe went inside. A secretary typed away, filling out forms, and Bob Knowles, the yard owner, manned the counter. Through a pane of glass behind his head, the sale ring could be seen as well as the small wood podium from which the auctioneer called the sale and directed his stewards to the buyers. Bob Knowles had been here since the years Joe and his family were still on the ranch. He peered at Joe with a smile.

"How long you back for this time?" he asked.

"Damned if I know. But Lureen lost her lease. I told her I'd watch some yearlings for her this summer. She had a grass deal with Overstreet and he dropped her. How's it look for today?"

"Dribs and drabs," said Bob, lifting his feed-store cap to smooth back his sandy hair. "All day long. What are you looking for?"

"Grass cattle, but everyone's got so much hay left over."

"That's it. We just don't have the numbers," Bob said. Joe completely trusted Bob and moreover, he didn't want to hang around here all day every Tuesday buying cattle ten at a time.

"Bob, you want to sort up some cattle for me and just buy me what you can? Then just lot them till we get a couple of semiloads."

"Tell me what you want."

"Big-frame fives and sixes for under sixty-five bucks a hundredweight. Sort them up so they look like a herd."

"That's a tall order. Maybe too tall. How many do you want?"

"Two hundred and fifty head and I'd take some spayed heifers in there if it had to be."

"I can't do it in one day," Bob said decisively.

"Can you do it over four weeks?"

"I can get pretty close."

"Let's do 'er then. I'll get my banking done. And don't hesitate to make me some *good* buys." By this point, Joe was enjoying himself so much he was just hollering at Bob and Bob was hollering back.

Imagine, thought Joe, a world in which you could trust a man to buy you a hundred fifty thousand pounds of beef with your checkbook when he is getting a commission. A particular instance of the free enterprise system running with a Stradivarian hum.

Darryl Burke, the banker, had known Joe so long and liked Joe so well and was so glad he was back in town that he would have liked to see him skip this business with the cows and, as he said, "orient his antenna to the twentieth century." Joe sat in his bright vice-president's cubicle surrounded by tremendous kodachromes of the surrounding countryside.

"Cut the shit and give me the money," Joe said. He enjoyed viewing Darryl in his suit because it gave him the curious ticklish surprise of time passing to see an old pal of the mountain streams and baseball diamonds actually beginning to blur into "the real world." Joe was without contempt for "the real world"; it merely astonished him that any of his old friends had actually succeeded in arriving there. Joe leaned over and said in a loud whisper, "Does your secretary actually believe this act of yours?"

Darryl grimaced and waved his hands around. He knew of course that life was a trick. But it wouldn't do to have the secretary find it out. Joe hated having to sit somewhat outside and spot the gambits. But he sustained a slight fear that whatever carried people into cubicles and suits would deprive him of his friends. There did seem to be a narrowing as life went on. An old fishing companion who threw the longest and most perfect loop of line had become a master of the backhoe. He dug foundations and sewer lines more exactly than the architects drew them on paper. He had become his backhoe. He either rode the backhoe or he drank beer and thought about perfecting his hands on the levers. He suffered from carpal tunneling. He was never out of work. His family had everything they needed as the beer helped him swell toward perfect conjunction with the yellow machine. Was this the same as the cowboy who was said to be part of his horse?

"I'm sure you know that we are not in good times for these ranches."

"Yes, I do," called Joe.

"Nationally, we're looking at a foreclosure every seven minutes. If your dad was here, God bless him, he'd tell you all about this."

"You know the old saying, it can't happen to me. Besides, it's Lureen's. I'm just the hired man."

Darryl groaned. "Some of these fellows slip off into the night with the machinery. I can't say that I blame them. The FHA is topsy-turvy. We're no different. We're having to go after some of our best operators. Incidentally, I know about Lureen's arrangement. I know all about this ranch. And anything you do, she's going to have to sign."

"Well, don't worry. I'm going to be doing so little. One Four-H kid can do more than I'm going to do with the place. I'll scatter these yearlings and ship in the fall. It's not even really ranching. Anyway, like I say, I just work for Lureen."

"As long as you understand that every move drives you deeper. Lureen's going to have to come in." It surprised Joe that everyone seemed to know the arrangement. They considered it Joe's place. Maybe more than he did.

Joe bent over the papers, making a show of studying them. "Your nose is whistling," he said to Darryl. "Control your greed." Darryl sighed. When Joe finished, he looked up and said, "Let 'er buck. I'm back in the cattle business."

"But you're happy," said Darryl with a kind of crazy smile. "That's it, you're happy."

Joe knew he was going to have to buy a horse. So, he skimmed a few hundred from the cattle pool and went way out north of town to see Bill Smithwick, who broke ranch horses and used to work for Joe's father. He lived down along a seasonal creek, a place just scratched into the mainly treeless, dun-colored and endless space. Red willows grew down the trifling watercourse; and alongside them, as though they were a grove of ancient oaks, Bill had placed his home. It was an old, old travel trailer shaped like a cough drop and swathed in black plastic sheeting to keep the wind out. A black iron pipe brought water by gravity down to the half of a propane tank that served as the water trough; it was primitive, but a bright stream of clean water ran continuously. He had a big pen for loose horses and a round breaking corral. It was the bare minimum but it was fairly neat with the hay stacked right, the lariats hung up, the saddles in a shed and the old Dodge Pow- erwagon actually parked rather than left. There was a born- again bumper sticker on the truck's bumper that said: "The game is fixed. The lamb will win. Be there."

Bill Smithwick stepped out of the trailer. He wore sus- penders over a white V-necked T-shirt and had a beat-up Stetson way on the back of his head like an old-timer. He was a tough-looking forty with white arms and sun-blackened hands.

"Well, God damn you anyway, you no-good sonofabitch," he barked in a penetrating hog-calling tenor.

"I'm back."

"To stay?"

"I'm just back."

"You want to come in?"

"It's not big enough in there."

Smithwick reached behind him and got a shirt. He pulled it on and came into the yard. He shook Joe's hand like he was pumping up a tire. "Hey, what's the deal on your old place? Them neighbors been rippin' your aunty off something awful."

"We took it back. I'm going to run some yearlings there, till I see what's what."

"You and your aunt?"

"No, me."

"Come on, Joe!" shouted Smithwick in the hog-calling voice.

"Really," said Joe, sincerely.

"You're running yearlings and you need a horse."

"Yup."

"What are you going to do with that no-good, low-bred, yellow-livered, whey-faced, faint-hearted Smitty?" Bill shouted.

"He's part of the cost of doing business on that particular ranch."

"I foller you now."

"What you got around here in the way of a broke horse?" Joe asked.

"Well, all grade horses. And no appaloosas! Know why the Indians liked appaloosas?"

"Why?"

"They was the only horses they could catch on foot. And by the time they rode their appaloosas to battle they was so mad it made them great warriors."

"I have four hundred dollars I will give for a gelding seven years of age or less that you say is a good horse."

"Done."

Joe looked off at the pen of loose horses. "What did I buy?"

"Your purchase is a five-year-old bay gelding with black points named Plumb Rude, a finished horse. He's as gentle as the burro Christ rode into Jerusalem. How about a dog?"

"Have one, a dilly."

"I got two I could let go. One's fifteen and one's sixteen. The sixteen's the mother of the fifteen. The fifteen's got a undescended testicle but not so's a man'd notice."

Joe gave him the four hundred, which he had already rolled up in his shirt pocket with an elastic around it. Smithwick stuck it in his back pocket next to his snoose can.

"Let's go look at him," said Smithwick. He pulled his lariat down and they walked to the bronc pen. Plumb Rude was in a bunch of eight horses, easily spotted by the way he was marked, and by his habit of walking sideways and pushing other horses out of his way. He wasn't very big.

Smithwick made a loop and pitched his houlihan. The rope seemed to drop out of the sky over the head of Plumb Rude. Smithwick drew the horse up to him with the rope. The horse must have been caught this way regularly; he didn't seem to mind. "Appear all right to you?" The gelding looked like a horse in a Mathew Brady photograph, long-headed, raw-boned, with sloped, hairy pasterns.

"Looks fine."

"He's a little cold backed but that ain't gonna bother you. Saddle him and let him stand for a few minutes and he'll never pitch with you. And he's hard mouthed 'cause I got hard hands! Haw!"

"Bill, I don't have a trailer. Can you drop him by when you get a minute?"

"Where'll I leave him, in your dad's old corrals there?"

"That'd be fine."

Smithwick turned around and put his hands on his hips and gazed at the pen of broncs. He was the very picture of what Joe took to be happiness. "Lemme see," Joe heard him say, "who am I gonna mug today?"

12

About a week later, the yearlings started coming in on partial loads, eastbound. They never could get it together to make up a whole semiload. Joe just had to pick them up as they arrived. The truckers left them at the stockyard in Deadrock and stuck the receipts and brand inspections under the door at the scale house. Joe went out there with a stock trailer in the evening and an old irrigator's cow dog he had borrowed for the day. The low buttes on the prairie to the north of the stockyards were ledged with hot weather shadows, and blackbirds were lined up on the top planks of the cattle pens. Joe's cattle were bunched around an automatic waterer at one end, a mixed batch of light grass cattle. Joe backed the trailer to a Powder River gate and used the dog to load the cattle. He closed the door and looked in along the slatted sides of the trailer where the wet muzzles pressed out. He took his time going back out the river road and hauled them right through the wire gate on the south pasture. He stopped and opened the trailer just at dark. A few yearlings craned and looked out into the space; then one turned and stood at the rear edge of the trailer looking down. The others crowded in front, bawled, and the one looking down jumped. After a pause, the rest poured out to look at the new world. They scattered and began to graze. Joe felt something inside him move out onto the grass with the cattle. It was thrilling to feel it come back.

The house was below the level of the immediate surrounding hills. Before sunrise, the tops of the cottonwoods lit up as though they were on fire, while the lower parts of the trees and their trunks continued to stand in the dark of night. Gradually, the conflagration moved downward, revealing the trees, and finally raced out along the ground, emblazoning the horizontal sides of the ranch buildings.

Into this bright scene came old man Overstreet on a bony little grulla mare, and wearing an overcoat. Alongside of him, a middle-aged man hurried to keep up. He was wearing hiking boots and a buffalo plaid shirt. Overstreet gazed around the buildings from his trotting horse until he spotted Joe.

"Joe, I'm tickled to death to see you back. This here is Mr. Prendergast of the town of Philadelphia, Pennsylvania." Joe shook Mr. Prendergast's hand. He had a horsy, eager, well-bred face. "Mr. Prendergast is writing about our area for . . . for what?"

"For a German travel magazine," said Mr. Prendergast.

"How are you, Mr. Overstreet?" Joe shook his hand. The old man had aged startlingly to a kind of papery fierceness like a hornet.

"Where's Otis Rosewell?" Joe asked.

"He rode a sedan to the bottom of the Gros Ventre River. Otis has been gone for years."

"I'm sure sorry to hear it." Joe was startled that he had never heard this before.

"I've been seeing these mixed cattle coming in. Who do they belong to?" Overstreet asked crossly.

"Really, they're Lureen's steers. I'm taking kind of a break. I told her I'd watch them for her."

"Why didn't she come to me?" Overstreet demanded.

"She said you had given up your lease."

"I had, I had! But I didn't expect her to cut off communications!"

"I don't think she meant to do that, Mr. Overstreet. But like I say, I was willing to watch them for her. And the grass was already coming."

"Let me tell you something, young man. This outfit sets slap in the middle of me. I would have had it long ago if it hadn't galled me to let your dad stick me up. But you people need to clear some of these ideas with me before you go off half cocked."

Joe was not happy with the phrase "you people."

"Mr. Overstreet," he said, "we don't need to do any such a thing."

"I'm only interested in what's neighborly," said Overstreet, turning to go. "That's how the West was won." Prendergast laughed uncomfortably and the two of them went off, Prendergast having to jog to the horse's walk as old man Overstreet shouted, "Prendergast, write that down!"

There was a dog living underneath the house, a mass of gray fur living in solitary misery. Joe had glimpsed it three different times, just at dusk when it sat on a low ridge, looking out over the empty country north of the ranch. He began to leave a pan of kibble on occasion to see if he couldn't get this dog to accommodate itself to some degree to the human life of the ranch. But it was pretty clear he was going to have to shoot it; skunks were showing up with rabies and an untended dog like this would be held responsible for all depredations on local livestock.

Joe sat on a nearby hill with a rifle watching the pan of dog food, often drifting off into a nap during which he inevitably had bad, guilty dreams about shooting the dog. It was a job Joe didn't want.

Once he shone the flashlight under the cabin. Exposed teeth glistened in its beam. The dog snarled without ever taking a breath, a continuous, bubbling drone. Joe could have shot it where it was. Getting the corpse out was one thing, but the idea of killing something which had retreated to a final crevice not one other creature desired was insupportable.

Sometimes Joe sat outside the cabin until the dog thought he had gone. Then he would hear the dog moaning to itself, a whimpering agony as its parasites gnawed away at it. Joe put a piece of meat on a pole and shoved it up under the cabin so that he could feel the jarring of the feeding dog, and its agony resumed like a great outside force.

He went to the vet and bought an aerosol can of boticide, antiseptic, and a pair of sheep shears. He now had forty-three dollars tied up in the dog. Then he bought a T-bone. That brought it to almost forty-nine. He drove out to the cabin.

When he played his light underneath the building, the wolf-ish eyes burned yellow. The dog growled on, both inhaling and exhaling. Around its face, a thick corona of matted fur extended for half a foot in all directions. Joe pushed a pole up in there at the end of which he had arranged a noose of broken lariat. The dog shuddered back to the ultimate inch of recess, driving dust forth in a swirl around the beam of light as the pole approached. It snapped with lightning speed at the end of the pole but the loop kept on coming forward until it was around the brute's neck. Joe tightened the loop slightly, then slipped the pole out. Now holding the nylon rope, he could feel the throb of life at its end. A peculiar quiet reigned in the dusty yard as Joe looked around in an attempt to foresee the consequence of pulling the creature into the light of day. Maybe the dog had the right idea. But Joe had grown up with dogs and this one had lost all shadow of the old alliance with mankind and had become an instrument of secrecy and fear.

The time had come. Joe began to pull. A scrambling could be heard from within and a faint dust cloud rolled out, accompanied by the most piteous tone, a pitch of voice rendingly universal. Joe was about to overwhelm all of the dog's accumulation of temper and habit and to drag him out into the daylight.

The rope was as hard as a stick in his hand. It yielded a degree at a time. Sweat poured from Joe. It runneled down his laugh lines. It stung his eyes. As the dog advanced to meet its fate, it occurred to Joe that he didn't know what it looked like, except for that big wedge of muzzle. For a split second, a part of him wondered what would happen if the dog weighed a thousand pounds. Joe regained enough rope to be able to coil it at his feet. He made one coil, then another, and while he was making the third, the dog shot out from under the cabin, hit the end of the rope and snatched Joe onto his face. Joe held on while the dog ran baying in a great circle, its hindquarters sunk low to scramble against the restraint of the rope.

Joe got to his feet with the rope still in his hands, his palms burned and stinging. He retreated until he reached a pine tree that once shaded the yard of the cabin. Here he was able to take a couple of turns around the base of the tree, and bracing his weight against the rope draw the dog to the tree and snub its head against it. Joe's heart ached at the suffering of the animal in its captivity, the misery which broad daylight seemed to bring. The dog lay there and howled.

Joe bound the dog's mouth shut with twine, narrowly avoiding being bitten, and began to clip the fur with the sheep shears. As soon as he broke the surface of the matted fur, he hit a bottomless layer of pale, thick maggots and felt his gorge rise. He drove back his loathing until he had clipped the dog from end to end, down to its festering skin. He got an old rusted gas can from the shadow of the cabin and went to the small creek that ran past to fill the can with water. He rinsed the dog over and over while the dog, thinking that it was drowning, renewed its moans. Once Joe was sure the dog was clean, he sprayed it with antiseptic and then finally a blast of aerosol with the botfly medicine. The dog lay panting.

Joe cut the twine binding the dog's mouth, placed the T-bone within reach and freed the rope. The pink medicated mass of the dog, whose wounded pride found voice in a sustained howl, bolted across the dirt yard past the eloquent T-bone and into the hayfield, where it sat and poured out a cry and lamentation for the life in the dark which it had lost.

Joe spent the rest of the morning sealing up the space underneath the cabin with rocks. The dog sat in the field and watched him, making small adjustments in its position toward the steak. Joe noticed these adjustments and, as he walked back toward the ranch, he felt that, given time, the dog would sell out. He thought he knew how the dog felt.

•

The phone rang. There was some excitement about getting his first call. A small voice came over the line. "Joe, this is Ellen Overstreet. Do you remember me?"

"Why I sure do. How are you, Ellen?"

"I'm just fine, Joe. I was excited to hear you were back."

"Where are you living these days?"

"Until recently, outside of Two Dot. But we're separated. I think we'll work it out though."

" 'We,' who is we?"

"Actually, I'm Ellen Kelton now. Do you remember Billy Kelton?"

"Are you kidding? After all the thumpings he gave me? Is he still the wild cowboy I remember?" Joe's question was polite in the extreme.

"Well, not nearly. He's gone to ranching."

"Are you all going to make it through this dry spell?"

"I honestly wonder," said Ellen in a musical voice. "We have had such dust pneumonia in our calves from following their mothers down these old cow trails to water. We've lost quite a few of them. Billy's spent all his time doctoring."

"I can't tell you how nice it is to hear your voice. It *sounds* like you're as pretty as ever."

"I'm not!" Ellen laughed. "On the other hand, nobody puts on weight around here. But let me get to the point."

"All right," Joe said warmly; but the truth was, a nervous feeling had invaded his stomach, something which had just crossed time from where he used to be to where he was now.

"I just thought—and I don't know how easy it will be to do—but I just thought you might like to see your daughter."

"*My* daughter? You say *my* daughter. Well, yes! What's her name?" Joe watched the wind toss an end of the curtain into the room. He knew what was meant when people talked about time stopping. He felt his hand moisten on the telephone receiver.

"Her name is Clara."

"Clara. Where did you get that?"

"It's Billy's mother's name."

"I see. Kind of an old-timey name. I guess I'm going to see her, huh?" A sudden intimacy descended with the crisis. "I mean, why in hell don't you just tell me what I'm supposed to do, Ellen."

"That's up to you, Joe. I'm just making the offer."

"Anybody know this?"

"I told Dad."

"You did? And what did he say?" His mouth had gone chalky. "You told your father?"

"He said, 'Good,' 'cause Clara will get it all when you people's place is part of his and it all makes a perfect square."

"Well, this just kind of floors me. And well, Ellen, what about you? What happened to your plans?"

"I teach. I teach at Clarendon Creek."

"That's where I went! That's where my Aunt Lureen taught."

"The first four grades."

Joe could smell the sweat pouring through his shirt. He felt like he was burning up. He felt as if the rickety logic of his new life had just disappeared.

"I would like to see her," Joe said. "Any arrangement that you would like suits me."

"I just wanted to find out if you were interested," she said in the same musical voice. "I'll be in touch!"

An old man named Alvie Butterfield who irrigated for the Overstreets came through the ranch yard to change the water in his head gate. He had with him the border collie Joe had used as his cattle came in. Alvie was on a small battered Japanese motorcycle wearing his hip boots. He had his shovel fastened down with bungee cord and his blue heeler balanced on the passenger seat. Joe was walking to the truck with a load of outgoing mail and stopped to talk. They ended up talking about Zane Grey. Alvie's old face wrinkled and his eyes looked off to unknown distances. He said, "I believe everything in them books. When them cowboys are in the desert, I'm hot. When they're caught in a blizzard I send the old lady for another blanket. When they run out of food, I tear down to the kitchen to make a peanut butter sandwich." Even recalling these moments with his nose in Zane Grey caused rapturous transformation in Alvie, and the reality of a life directing muddy water downhill was made tolerable.

"I'm supposed to put out new salt," said Alvie, "but I'm too goddamn tired. You wouldn't think about doing that for me, would you?"

"Sure I would," Joe said.

"You can still find your way around up there, can't you?"

"I think so," said Joe.

"I'm mighty grateful," Alvie said. "Like I say, I'm wore out."

Alvie wandered up the creek and Joe loaded the truck with blocks of salt. He drove up through the basin, got out to lock the hubs, put it in four-wheel drive and climbed into the clouds, passing the Indian caves and the homesteaders' coal mine, before he tipped over into the summer pasture. There were cattle scattered out on the hills in all directions. He could just make out the three small white structures of the salt houses in the blue distance. A velvet-horned mule deer ambled out through the deep grass ahead of him and bluebirds paused on the cedar fenceposts. The only sign of human life was an old sheep shearing engine abandoned half a century ago and looking in the dry air as though it would still run. It was vanity to think about owning this sort of thing. Joe could not exactly understand property. We want things when others want the same things. Still, looking out at pastures that ran to threadlike rivers at eye level, Joe could feel his bones blowing in the wind of the future, and it was a cheerful feeling. All his feelings were currently askew because of Ellen's call, but this was still a good one.

He loaded all the salt out and checked the two main springs. One was reduced in volume because of the winter's low snowpack at the heads of the coulees, but the cattle were still using it. The northern fence line was barely standing, held up by the sagebrush through which it ran, but it held all right and nothing seemed to be going through it. Joe had built that fence. When cattle got out, they just drifted into space and it was an easy thing to get them back in. There was grass everywhere, even on top of the wind-blown ridges where he and Otis had dynamited fencepost holes so long ago. He remembered now what a good gaining pasture it was and how his father, who was a grass man, used to say, Just take care of it and it will take care of you.

He left the truck and walked. The pasture lay in three broadly defined planes that tilted separately and disappeared into the sky. He walked toward a tall rock formation that had once figured in a dream of his boyhood, a dream he had never quite figured out as to all its sources and details and implied perils. But this dream had left him with a high degree of respect for the operations of the subconscious.

In his twenties, many years after the rock episode, he had eaten peyote and had the pleasure of a long conversation with thousands of irises, tulips, and roses at a commercial flower garden. He could *still* remember their nodding concern at each of his questions, their earnest weaving around on the ends of their stalks. As ridiculous as this experience came to seem, it enlarged his respect for flowers; and he sometimes found himself entering someone's property with a sidelong and deferential nod to the garden.

When he reached the great banded rock chimney, something went through him with a signifying interior chime as powerful as looking at an empty bed where a parent once died. A cloud of birds set forth into the wind. Joe sat down and let himself go back.

Joe's nearest neighbor of his own age had been Billy Kelton, already a great big strong boy who was, in those days long before the family moved to Minnesota, Joe's best friend. Billy's father owned the Hawkwood Store. The two boys both had part-time jobs during the school year and ranch jobs in the summer. One day, when they were both thirteen, Billy had come to visit Joe and they got into an argument pitching horseshoes. Joe's father came out and said, "You'd better settle this like men." Joe didn't think he had a chance, and while he stalled Billy sensed not only the opportunity but the peculiar energy coming to him from Joe's father. He landed a roundhouse blow in Joe's face that bloodied him and brought him to his knees. Joe's father ordered Joe to his feet, but when he stood Billy flattened him with a blow to his right ear that sent pain and shame scalding across his vision. A roaring noise seemed to come up around him. Through it all, he could hear his father cheering Billy on. He looked up and saw his father's incredible animation as he shoved the suddenly reluctant Billy toward his son's collapsed form. Even now the memory was terrible.

Joe's father had said, "You'll think about this for a long time. You'll think about what people are really like. That wasn't your enemy that did that to you. That was supposed to be your friend. You think about that just as hard as you can."

Joe ran away that day just long enough to climb to this pasture. He came straight to the banded rock chimney where he sat down and wept for his defeat, wept for his father's collusion in his defeat, wept for the loss of a friend, and the feeling which he never quite ever again escaped that life had as one of its constant characteristics a strain of unbearable loneliness.

As far as he was from the house, he still felt too exposed to the world that day. He touched the altered shapes of his face with his fingertips. Beneath the striped rock was a deep fissure, like a small cave, and Joe crawled into it and lay down in the cool dark. Peace came over him and, as he began to sleep, he plummeted into a dreamy abyss.

Indians poured out of the base of the rock and Joe was one of them. They were anonymous in paint and dyed porcupine quills and trade bead chokers, behind shields illuminated with the shapes of eternity. They moved like a school of fish and swarmed up on their horses. Concentric red circles of ochre were painted around the eyes of Joe's horse and its body was covered by the outlines of human hands. He rested his lance against the horse's neck. The raven feather tied at the base of its point fluttered against the shaft as they galloped over the rims to the small valley below where the white people had built their cabins. Though it was his family's home, Joe could not even remember it in the dream. A man and a woman ran out to meet them, to try to talk; they were blurred unrecognizably by the direct glare of the sun. It was too late for talk. The Indians rode right over the white people in a sudden tension of bows and sailing of arrows and lances. The dust from the horses settled slowly on their absence. The buildings burned as sudden as phosphorus, sparkled and were gone. Everything was gone. Even the stony white of foundations and bones was gone. The wild grass resumed its old cadence.

Joe's mother watched closely over the days it took for the swelling to subside in his face. She let this concern speak for itself and carefully avoided any discussion of the event. Joe said nothing either, though whatever was in the air seemed strong enough. Finally, when only the greenish shadow of a bruise at his temple remained, she asked without seeming to expect an answer, "Your father has made a pretty big mistake with you, hasn't he?"

He didn't answer. He just stared in silence and let her work her way through her changed allegiance.

14

His first free afternoon, Joe stopped by the Clarendon Creek school. Ellen stood on the edge of the small clearing that served as a playground, her sweater tied around her waist and wearing a pair of tennis shoes so that she could double as a physical education instructor. She was urging four tiny children in running laps out around a two-story boulder and back. Their books and papers were weighted with stones next to the lilacs.

"Hi there," Ellen said with an enormous smile.

"What do you know about this?"

"It's pretty wild," she said.

"I couldn't wait."

"You're looking well, Joe."

"Thanks. And you."

"Do you mean it?"

"I do."

"How's your painting?"

"I'm in the space program actually."

"What a shame. You used to write to me from school, remember? About your painting. You were going to be a new Charlie Russell. I saw one of your paintings finally. I really couldn't understand it, Joe. It looked kind of like custard. Next to a house, sort of."

"That happens to belong to one of the Rockefellers," Joe said defensively, but the name, he saw, didn't ring a bell.

"Let me make it quick. I've got to go back inside. Clara is with her dad this month."

"On the same old Kelton place?" Joe asked, feeling awkward.

"Yes, but don't go there. I'll try to work something out. And look, please be discreet. Billy is a wonderful father and I don't want to disturb that."

"How about dinner?"

"You what?"

"Would you like to have dinner?" he asked.

"Your face is red!"

"Nevertheless, the invitation stands."

"Yes!" The four children completed their lap and Ellen drifted toward the schoolhouse with them. "Call!" she said. "For directions. We can have a scandal!"

He recognized that there was an unworthy basis to his extreme present happiness. His life was taking a turn that would help push Astrid out once and for all. He already felt the freshness and the simplicity of Ellen as an antidote, though he semi-admitted to himself that that was not what people were for.

He picked Ellen up at six, at her apartment. The length of day had advanced so that it seemed the middle of the afternoon. She came down the outside stairway, skittering to the ground level, looking as fresh as though it were first thing in the morning, in a dark blue summer dress with minute white stars. She had braided her mahogany-colored hair and pinned it up.

"I'm starving," she said, inside the car. "I got so wound up talking to the children about Lewis and Clark I must have burned a lot of calories. I had fun trying to make them see the part of the expedition that went up the Missouri. I tried to make them realize that for Lewis and Clark it was like going into space. I told them the Missouri was the great highway for the Indians and all the tributaries were neighborhoods with different languages and different histories. The little turkeys would really rather hear about war but the unknown gives them a shiver too. Or what they all call 'the olden days.' I'm going to split the difference with them. I'll show them Clark's camp on the Yellowstone and then take them over near Grey-cliff to the graves where the Blackfeet massacred Reverend Thomas and his nephew. By the way, I'm learning to play golf. I'm going through a difficult time and about a hundred people have recommended golf. I'm glad they did. By the second lesson, I preferred golf to marriage!"

Joe looked at her as long as he thought he could. What a feeling this was giving him! He was driving through a nice neighborhood. In one yard, a man shot around his lawn on a riding mower in high gear. At the next house, an old gent stood in the opening of a well-kept garage with its carefully hung collection of lawn tools on the wall behind him. On most lawns, a tiny white newspaper lay like a seed. American flags cracked from the porches. On the last lawn before Main Street, a rabbit sat between two solemn children.

They walked into the lobby of the old Bellwood Hotel. The bar off to the left was full of after-work customers. Two cowboys came out with their drinks to have a look at Ellen while they waited for their table. "Yes?" she said in her best schoolteacher's manner. They shot back inside.

"I'll have the sixteen-ounce rib-eye," said Ellen before she'd had a look at the menu. The waitress came and took their drink orders: a draft beer for Joe, Jim Beam on the rocks for Ellen. Joe decided on some pan-fried chicken and ordered for both of them. The dining room was half full. A schoolteacher was kind of a celebrity in a small town like this, so they got a few glances. It was too soon for anyone to have put much else together.

Joe was trying hard to relate the present confident Ellen to the early version he had known. He felt he had to do it quickly because the present Ellen would soon eradicate the one he remembered.

"Someone told me you people were getting ready to lose the place," said Ellen. "Dad keeps trying to figure out how to get it. He's only been doing that for forty years."

"It's hard to say."

"Although I don't know what good a ranch is anymore. My dad has been getting jailbirds to help put up hay because they're the only people desperate enough to work. To get somebody to fence you have to find an alky who wants to be in the hills to dry out. Plus the grasshoppers and Mormon crickets are about half ridiculous. I think my dad might just go to town. I don't blame him."

Joe listened intently. It gave him a chance to stare at her without having to talk. He knew Overstreet would never go to town.

"By the way," she said, "let me ask you this, okay? Don't you have a girlfriend?"

"I did."

"Well?"

"She died in a fern bar stampede."

A look of tolerance crossed Ellen's face. Joe tried to re-member Astrid charitably but all that came up was her push-iness, her health fetishes, her fascination with cosmetics. Astrid had taught him the field strategy for the aptly named war of the sexes. She had also taught him the charm and drama of picnics on the battlefield. It was a provisional life with this Astrid.

Ellen was as good as her word. When the meals came, she made short work of her big steak. Once when her mouth was too full, she grinned straight at Joe, and shrugged cheerily. This appetite amazed him. And when she was done, she flung herself back in her seat and said, "Ah!"

"Now what?" said Joe, putting down his own utensils. He was thinking about a cigarette. The tension of not mentioning the child was getting sharper.

"Would you like a suggestion?"

"Sure."

"I'd like to go out to Nitevue and hit a bucket of balls."

"I'd rather talk about Clara."

"I'd rather hit a bucket of balls."

They were the only two people on the range. It was a green band in the middle of prairie, glowing under floodlights. Nite-vue was situated just off the highway east. It was an open shed with places to sit, three soft drink machines, a golf cart, and a small counter where one arranged for the clubs and balls. Ellen asked for a number-four wood and Joe asked for anything that was handy, which turned out to be a thing called a "sand iron." The concessionaire looked just like a local farmer in a John Deere cap and overalls. He made it clear in every movement that his class background had taught him to despise all sport and waste such as this. He handed over balls, clubs, and tees with an air of ancient loathing.

Ellen stood up on a kind of rubber mat and began firing the balls out through the bug-filled flood of light, almost to the darkness beyond. At first Joe just watched her. There were gophers speeding around, running, stopping, looking, whistling, trying to fathom life on a driving range.

Joe took three whiffs for every time he hit the ball. But even when he did connect, it just went up at a high angle and landed a short distance away. He took a somewhat mightier grip and swung hard; this time the ball almost towered out of sight, yet fell just in front of them. Quickly absorbing the spirit of this unusual game, he shouted, "Sonofabitch!" and examined the end of his club for manufacturing deficiencies. He went back and demanded another club; this one was a "two iron." With it, he managed to scuff the ball along the ground in front of himself, while Ellen drove one long clean shot after another. What's more, his arms ached from inadvertently fetching the ground itself blow after blow.

When she had finished driving her last ball, Ellen walked over to where Joe was sitting on a bench. Her cheeks were flushed with high spirits. Joe thought that it would be a very strange individual who didn't find her lovely.

"You don't seem to have much of a gift for this," she said.

"I'm afraid I don't. Actually, I tried it a few years back. I'm about the same. My dad took it up late in life. I always found something sad in that. Couldn't put my finger on it."

"Tell you what, why don't you drop me at my place. I've got papers to correct and I make an early start. Probably by the time you get out of bed, I've been hitting a lick for two hours."

Joe took a leisurely drive along the river and then turned up her street. There just didn't seem to be any pressure anywhere. When they reached her house, he walked her to the bottom of the outside stairs to her apartment. She turned suddenly, reached to one of his hands, gave it a kind of rough squeeze, bounded up the stairs—"I enjoyed it!"—and was gone behind her door. He stood there vaguely happy, vaguely conscious that they had never made a real plan to see his daughter. He was ashamed to admit that it seemed too much. And the mention of Billy Kelton as a good father galled him.

15

The great window in the front room hung halfway
open, the iron sash weights visible in their wooden channels.
Cliff swallows ascended to their mud nests under the deep
eaves of the old house. Joe thought, Man, I'm getting lone-
some; let's have a look at the young people. There were times
when the views from his windows seemed full of undisclosed
meaning, of tales waiting to unfold. But today their views were
as flat as reproductions. He had a tubular glass bird feeder
hung outside the sitting room window and the seeds it had
scattered on the sill just seemed unkempt. The birds didn't
seem to care if they ate or not. He looked at the phone and
it rested in its place as though its days as an instrument were
finished. He felt there was nothing for him to do. Whatever
was next, he hadn't started. His old life smothered him.

He took the highway east over the foothills, passing a spot
where you could shoot a buffalo and put it on your credit card.
When he stopped for gas, a boy cleaned his windshield and
poured out his heart to Joe. He said that his mother had been

married more than ten times and that he and his brother had lived in nineteen cities. The boy couldn't remember the names of all the husbands but said, "We had to call every one of them sonsofbitches 'Daddy.' " All Joe could think of was good solid ways of putting his old life to an end.

While the youngster cleaned the windshield and checked under the hood, Joe used the pay phone. It was late in New York.

"Ivan, hi, it's Joe."

There was a long pause. Joe pictured Ivan in his bathrobe, his thick, effective shape like that of a veteran football lineman, characteristically pressing a thumb and forefinger into his eye sockets.

"Why are you calling me in the middle of the night?"

"Because I need to see you."

"I don't like this, Joe."

"Will you see me?"

"Of course I'll see you. Where are you?"

"Montana."

"*Look Homeward, Angel.*"

"Sort of."

"Find what you expected?"

"More."

"How did you leave off with Astrid?"

"I just flew the coop, adiosed it. I don't feel too good about that, actually."

"I'll check in with her."

"So, if you tell me it's okay, I'm coming."

"Sure it's okay. Are you a cowboy again?"

"You know, Ivan, I sort of am."

"It's a riot," said Ivan.

•

Joe slept all the way to La Guardia. After missing the whole night on the ranch, he watched the sun rise over the Atlantic Ocean.

He took a cab into the city, his small duffel bag on the seat beside him. The skyline of New York, with his cab pointed straight at it, filled Joe with excitement. The unpronounceable name on the cabbie's license, the criminal style photograph, the statement on the grill that separated him from his passengers about his having less than five dollars in change, the omnipresent signs of crowd control measures excited Joe beyond words. Protected by their cars, motorists boldly exchanged glances on the freeway.

He checked into the Yale Club. The lobby was full of younger graduates and their dates. There was a wine tasting announced on a placard in the lobby and a Macanudo cigar sampling in the Tap Room. There were new regulations about jogging clothes in the lobby. There were serious conversationalists around the elevators and two harried bellhops with mountains of luggage on their carts. Four Southerners in their early thirties hooted and pounded one another. "Anybody catch the secretary of commerce doin' his little numbah on the TV?" asked one lanky young man in a Delta drawl. When neither of his fellows answered him, a tight-faced man at the next elevator did. "I saw him," he said, "and he was right on the money." There weren't usually this many young people around. It was a yuppie *Brigadoon*.

Joe carried his own bag to his room, walking down a hallway hung with crew pictures and ambulance-service citations from the First World War. Three Filipino maids chatted in the open doorway of a linen closet, greeting him as he passed. His room was really good, like a room in an old home, though he had to sidle around the bed to clear the dresser, the radiator, and the writing desk. The room had a wooden smell. Joe remembered staying here when he was in school, riding down from New Haven on the train along the seaboard of battered buildings and grassless lots; sometimes he caught glimpses of the exhausted ocean or the odd things that had been thrown out, old window frames, a child's toy bugle, wired bundles of newspapers, cars parked so long their tires were flat, all of which used to stir Joe. Sometimes it seemed superior to the space and quiet of the West.

Leaving his bag unopened on the bed, he went downstairs, back through the lobby and across to Grand Central Station. He walked down into the vast hall of railroading to buy a newspaper. He stared at the schedule boards overhead and noted that it was still unbelievably possible to go to White Plains.

He decided he would walk for a while. Still amazed at the unreturned glances of the crowd, he felt himself swept against the windows of the shops. He felt a growing desire to be better dressed. He sympathized with the men selling stolen and counterfeit goods from the curb; he thought it must take an exceptional individual to wrest himself from the anomie and become a customer. When cars were stopped in the inter-sections by traffic signals, he trusted the pattern of his fellow humans in pouring through the narrow gaps between bump-ers. Yet it was hard to forget that with a slip of the clutch one was legless. Part of his sense of liberation in New York was the impression of human volume and the consequent trivial-ization of his problems. If an individual ran out into the crowd from a doctor's office to shout, "I've just found out I have cancer!" it wouldn't have much effect. New York really took the pressure off the basics and Joe felt this liberation in his buoyant stride, his desire to be better dressed, and his inclination to try the cuisines of all peoples. His single year of life in the city taught him that fun at sex, there for the asking, was the steady undertone. Its utilitarian savor ran the risk of all pleasantries.

"The trouble is," said his then roommate, Ivan Slater, after a year of this, "you end up buying them a fifty-dollar dinner. And the more indistinguishable they get, the more it's like having some show dog in your pants that can't live on ordinary kibble."

"Stop!" Joe said. "Stop!"

His room was on the ninth floor but he mistakenly took the elevator to the seventh, got off, and had to press the call button and wait once again. A woman in her early thirties came along and pressed the down button.

"Hi," said Joe. She had a sunny, outdoors look and wore a green-checked dress that suited her pretty figure.

"How are you?"

"I pressed the wrong button."

"You mean you're going down?"

"No, I mean in the lobby. I meant to get off at nine."

"Your face is red," she said.

He said, "I'm lonely."

They had leapt through layers of intimacy with this exchange. He could have said anything. He could have asked her to have sex with him and gotten an uncomplicated yes or no response. But an elevator arrived, and she stepped aboard, saying, "Ta-ta." Presently, his own elevator came and he was on his way to his room. His message light was on. How had she gotten his room number? But it was only Ivan confirming their dinner hour. He stretched out and watched television for a while. His bones ached. He let his mind follow the sirens from the street below. He imagined living here and the thought was a happy one. He could go upstairs to the library or take squash lessons. He could breakfast here every morning before venturing into the street. Finally, a kind of sight which lay buried inside him, stunned to blindness not only by open country but by the sea, would awaken to something he never could have predicted. And he would choose to depict it. Out would come the brushes and paint. Dab, dab, dab.

Joe put on a clean shirt and a blue-and-green-striped silk tie. His suit jacket was rumpled but it was of such acceptable tailoring that he thought it made him look either hard-working or scholarly. He rather liked the figure he cut. When he got to the foyer of the dining room on the twenty-second floor a few minutes before eight, the girl from the seventh floor was there waiting for a table by herself.

"So, we meet again," he said, a remark so deplorable to him that he immediately understood why she furrowed her brow and smiled formulaically. The intimacy of a short time ago was withdrawn. "So sorry." The smile changed and became genuine. She turned her wonderful almost Mediterranean face to one side and regarded him. She is about to ask me something, and something big, he thought. She may ask me if I'd like a loan. I don't know yet but soon I will.

The silver doors of the elevator opened and Ivan Slater stepped out, wearing the latest Italian fashions, wide shoulders, a kind of one-button roll, really an old-fashioned hoodlum suit but made in the bright shades of a discount carpet barn. The shirt was green and the tie was red. He wore great spatulate suede shoes and his pants were held up by what appeared to be a pajama string. His proximity to the fashion centers entitled him to spend a fortune to look like a fool.

Ivan's round, pumpkinlike head and piercing black eyes seemed to say "Stop the music!" while he regarded his illustrator. Joe remembered when he and Astrid used to stay in New York at Ivan's apartment, making love by the second-floor glow of streetlights, mantis shadows climbing the walls.

"Hold it right there," said Joe, turning to the young woman. "You were saying?"

"I was saying?"

"Weren't you about to say something?"

"I wasn't but I will if you like. I can see you'd like me to."

Ivan, watching close, pounded Joe on the back with a sharp laugh. "I see you haven't lost any of your speed," he said in a voice that swung the headwaiter around from the middle of the dining room. "Not you," Ivan called to the headwaiter, jabbing a finger up and down in midair over Joe's head. "*Him.*"

When the headwaiter came, Joe deferred to the lady. She said she was waiting for someone. Joe and Ivan took a table near the middle of the room and Ivan ordered a margarita and buried his face in the menu. Joe asked for a bourbon and water, thinking it seemed like a vaguely out-of-town drink.

"I can't wait to hear about what you've done for Miss X," said Ivan from behind the menu. Joe was baffled: he thought Miss X was dead in the water.

Right after the drinks arrived, the young lady came to her table, the next one over, by herself. "I've been stood up," she said and grinned. She pulled the corners of her mouth down in a sad-face. Joe shook his head sympathetically and insincerely. Then her embarrassment looked real, the sort of vulnerability one galloped into like a hussar.

While they drank and waited for the waiter to take their dinner order, Ivan brought Joe up to date on the manufacturing problems he had hurdled since they last met. Some of them were quite considerable, having to do with separate manufacturers using different quality-control procedures for each of the components, so that holy terrors existed at the assembly end. With Ivan, personnel matters tended to be "love feasts" while manufacturing matters were "blood baths." Ivan had been through this before on simpler things and with purely industrial products involving robotics in the garment industry, which had made him unpopular but had made him money while putting others out of work. But this time it was different. This time it was a blood bath disguised as a love feast. To offset its effect, he said, "What made you want to go back to Montana?"

"Nothing else seems to be home."

"Is that important?"

"It is to me."

"At this point, right?"

"I think it's generally important," said Joe.

"Aw, bullshit," said Ivan. " 'Home' is a concept whose importance rises when people are down in the mouth. Healthy minds don't give a big rat's ass whose country they're even in. How's my friend Astrid?"

"She hasn't seen fit to join me as yet."

Ivan and Astrid frequently spoke on the telephone and even wrote letters. They would have made an ideal elderly couple. Joe sometimes wondered whether it was only sarcastic brutes like Astrid and Ivan who could rise to uncomplicated fondness.

The soup came, saffron chicken. Joe dipped his spoon in it. Ivan looked quite crumpled in his fashions of the hour. By sitting in his slumped position he caused the shoulders of his jacket to stand straight out beneath his ears. Industrial leadership from this man seemed out of the question. The well-bred diners all around them paused to look twice at Ivan, though as he himself would be quick to point out he could easily buy and sell any one of them. Their vague curiosity was felt by Joe as a pressure. He had seen Ivan burst into a chorus of "I'll-buy-you's" before and it wasn't pretty.

Joe had ordered a piece of scrod and a dinner salad. Ivan had ordered a steak, after inquiring which one was the biggest. Their meals came and this seemed to cheer him. In fact, after a brief moment's thought, Ivan seemed to be emotionally restored. Ivan was a hearty, life-loving man, and it wasn't long before he was greedily passing hunks of steak into his mouth. He had to raise and lower his eyebrows with every mouthful to show how good it tasted. A shadow crossed his features while he thought about death, or so Joe assumed.

"The key to me," Ivan said, "is solitude. I have no family. If I had children, all would be different. I've always known that. Alas, my personal miniseries is somewhat different. I continue my wolfish roaming in the capitalist forest. Indeed, right now, I'm having a big love feast with the Chinese. They're our kind of guys. No malarkey about work being their only natural resource, as per the Japanese. In their plant management practices, they do not live in romantic illusions about inventory control. I greatly prefer them to Japs. Japs are racists. Japs like to set you up in business so they can later steal whatever business you capture. But now the Japs are growing hubristic. Their society is changing. Their kids are narcissistic pukes like ours are. They think they can kick back and take it easy but they don't have the resource cushion that permits Americans to take dope, watch TV, and get out of shape. As soon as they lose a couple of steps of that big speed, their former allies are going to call in their marks. Meanwhile, the Chinks are in the passing lane with their balanced attitude, their cultural depth, their emerging talents, the scum of communism just beginning to be rinsed from their eyes"—the sedate dining room was quite concentrated on Ivan now—

"and they're looking across the Sea of Japan at their ancestral enemies and crying out, 'ALL RIGHT YOU FUCKIN' SLANTS, STAND BACK FROM YOUR TELEVISION SETS! WE CHINKS ARE GOING TO WHIP YOUR FUCKIN' ASSES!'" People stopped eating.

Ivan put a huge piece of steak in his mouth and all at once turned blue. Joe gazed at him a long time before noticing the color change, so great was his relief at the pause in his speech. The girl at the next table stared at Ivan.

"Is he all right?" she asked. "He's blue."

At that point, Ivan struggled to his feet and holding his throat, began making a sound like a seagull. Joe understood then that a piece of steak had lodged in his throat. Ivan started to stagger through the tables of diners before Joe could catch up to him. Joe knew the Heimlich maneuver and got behind Ivan, taking him around the waist below the rib cage and giving him as powerful a squeeze as his considerable strength would allow. Joe saw he had been successful even from this vantage point by the way the old Yalies jumped back from their tables. The thick bolus of beef, trailed by a yellow wing of vomit, flew across a couple of tables, and that was that. A dozen diners who had been seated were now standing, holding their napkins.

"Good as new!" crowed Ivan, returning to their table. But Joe could tell that he was deeply embarrassed. Suddenly, his thick frame in the latest fashions seemed less bold than sad. Ivan peered around from under his brows and saw that they were all still discussing him. He finally sat silent, smoldering, looking straight out at the diners now.

"That can kill you, y'know. Maybe those goddamn blue-blooded geeks don't know that. Maybe coupon clipping has kept them from learning that," he said in a piercing voice. Turning to Joe, he said, "Let's get a drink and the check."

The waiter danced over at the first signal. He was able to make a minor modification of the bill and leave it immediately. Joe signed it and slipped it under his water glass.

"Ivan, the reason I came to town was to tell you, face to face, that I'm not going to do the project. I'm not going to work with you anymore."

"I know, Joe."

"Oh."

"You told me a long time ago," said Ivan, "that you were getting out of real art so that you could come to feel as replaceable as the next guy."

"Yeah . . . ?"

"Well, you were right." Ivan got to his feet. "You're replaceable. All the luck in the world to you, Joe." Ivan was probably the closest thing to a real friend Joe had ever had. These words stung. Ivan stood up and went straight out, shedding his discomfort with every step. Joe rested his head in his hands, staring at a few square inches of tablecloth. When he lifted his head, he felt dizzy for just a moment. But when his eyes cleared, there was the girl at the next table.

"Join me for a drink?" she said. He looked at her clearly. She was beautiful.

"I'm sorry," said Joe, "but I'm afraid I don't know you."

She looked at him and smiled. She said, "What a relief!"

16

Joe and Ellen sat in the park, across from the drinking fountains, under a great blue Norway spruce.

"What's the problem?" Joe asked, brow furrowed in concern like some state-funded psychologist on autopilot. Ellen scrutinized him dubiously for a moment.

"I don't honestly know," she said. "But we've darn sure hit a fork in the road. Billy's had a tremendous amount of problems. After you left, he went in the Marines. He just seems to want to ranch, period, out in the hills doing his thing. And me, I'm about as quick to show sympathy over this Vietnam business as anybody. But it's not real cheerful, the way he goes about it. And like I say, he was in the Marine Corps and it seems to have started there. Being called maggots and stuff when they're just kids."

"Was he in some kind of combat?"

"Uh-huh."

"Do you still see him regularly?"

"We confine it strictly to matters concerning Clara. I don't encourage him. I finally put one of those little observation holes in my door, like an apartment. I had to put it in there because of Billy. Maybe I shouldn't say anything. My mother is seventy years old. She drives all the way in from the ranch to see me. I find myself looking at her through the little eyehole while she stands there with something she baked for me in her arms."

"What about when you want to see Clara?"

"Are you asking why she doesn't stay here with me in the apartment?"

"No, not at all," said Joe. He could see she was getting angry.

"Don't you think it's a little small? Don't you think I work hard enough?"

"No, I—"

"Have you ever heard of latchkey kids?"

"Yes, and that's not at all what I was talking about," Joe said. "I just thought this was a place I could see her. The ranch, with Billy and everything, isn't ideal."

"You're just going to have to be patient," Ellen said, then after a moment added, "I've still got an hour."

They dropped Ellen's books in the return slot at the library and went on with their stroll. Joe felt a strange tension in his stomach, the kind of thing that is communicated. They walked perhaps a block and the lack of a plan was creating enormous pressure.

"Let's go to my place," said Ellen quietly. It nearly paralyzed Joe. Her house was about three blocks away. Since he couldn't quite speak, he tried subtly changing his course. He could see the shiny auburn top of Ellen's head, the tan, freckled bands on the tops of her cheekbones. His agony lasted only the half a block of progress it took to confirm that that indeed was where they were headed.

A nerve-shattering cocker spaniel jolted toward them on four stiff legs attempting to turn itself inside out with a paroxysm of barking. They tried to ignore it, but the dog stole up from behind to bite. Joe turned around and kicked at it as the owner in a V-necked white T-shirt came out in the yard. "You want a cop?" yelled the owner. "Kick the dog and I get you a cop." The dog yelped back to the owner as though injured. Joe kept moving, though he felt his posture had rather collapsed. "Go on," bellowed the owner, "make my day!" But the next block took them into a quieter place where clothes billowed on a line and radios played merrily on windowsills.

The house Ellen lived in could be seen over neighboring rooftops a full block away. As they approached, it seemed to rise and enlarge.

"Come on up, it's unlocked," said Ellen. As she went up ahead of him, he was relieved to detect a lascivious thought at the angular motions of her hips under the cotton dress. What if I didn't have a lascivious thought? he wondered. What if I only thought of that character I met in Miami who burst into an Irish brogue at the moment of penetration? What a relief I'm not thinking of her! The "character" he was thinking about had been fascinated by her own Irish heritage and, during lovemaking, had cried, "Joe me lad, give it yer all!" He had never really gotten over it.

All he could think of was the character with the Irish brogue. He clutched the handrail as Ellen disappeared into her doorway. Good Christ. If I blow this one, I'll hang myself. I must turn into a wolf this minute or I'm lost; crude groping is the only thing that can get me beyond this impasse.

"Joe, what's holding you up?"

"Something in my shoe . . ." He sat on the stairs with his shoe in both hands, shaking it madly. "Just slip out of your little things and I'll be with you in a moment," he said in a gruff voice.

Ellen reappeared on the landing. "You what?" Joe was close to the limits of his endurance. He felt the flood building.

He rolled stomach-down onto the steps and let the laughter burst through him. He felt desperate as it ripped across his mind like a fire. He felt Ellen sit beside him.

"You know something?" she said in an admiring tone. "That's really funny, it really is. Are you all right?" Calmness began to pass over him, slowly, then it took hold. They agreed. It was funny. He was covered with sweat. He staggered to his feet, coming back to the world from an enormous distance. He could take her hand with simplicity. They could agree on going into her place.

"Here I fuck her brains out!" came the thought and he was on his stomach again.

"Joe, the neighbors are going to think you've flipped." He kept laughing. I'd just like to get me a little, was his final thought, recited in the decade-old voice of Slater as she stepped over his convulsed body and went back to work.

He didn't really want to think about the source of these hysterics. He knew down inside it was Astrid. She was using that santería on him from afar, that Cuban voodoo. She had left her prints in his mind and they weren't to be removed that easily. He did feel foolish. He felt that way for a week. He didn't try to see anyone. He didn't want to overdo his certainty about the cause of all this inadequacy. Then Ellen came on Saturday and took him touring. They went west for a couple of hours, with the sun behind them, in her car. She pretty much took the situation in hand; she got the room and they made love very happily. She didn't come across to him as starved or needy but a strong appetite was very evident. He was more used to the intricacies of staging and circumstance.

They were driving home in a distinct aftermath. Joe turned onto the main highway, bearing his palm down on the wheel and giving it a stylish whirl.

"Is this a good time to talk about Clara?" Joe asked.

"No, it is not."

The weather vacillated between blowing rain and infrequent openings of the sky to a higher world. Along the lower Madison, the hills angled toward the southeast were reared up into the oncoming weather and the wet clouds hung over the lower mesas and plateaus near the channels of the river. A cement truck labored along the frontage road.

Then the sun came out and in a short time there was not a cloud in the sky. But the road was still soaking wet and the car filled with the smell of rain and summer.

"I just can't understand why I did that," said Ellen, "when I'm trying to make a sincere effort to save my marriage."

They drove on for a while. Joe turned on the radio but it immediately seemed offensive and he shut it off. There was a great long bench at the south end of the Crazy Mountains that looked like a partly opened scallop shell. You could see all the blue of haze and sage and ditch-burning from here and minute sparkles of runoff from a distance, water carrying everything downward.

"Stop someplace," Ellen said, "I want to do it again." Joe took the first ranch exit and spiraled up above the interstate until he could see out in all directions for miles. The wind had the grass laid flat and a band of antelope drifted like a shadow of clouds. They undid each other's clothes and Joe slid toward her away from the wheel. She straddled him and pulled him into herself. "Jesus," she said, "I can't seem to stop."

There was a delicious grotesquery as she pounded into him. He could see his hair and forehead in the rearview mirror jarring with her motion. He was being levitated. He couldn't keep his eyes off the sky, the distance, out of his memories. "Watch my face," she said. Her eyes seemed to close and sink as he joined her. He felt a wet circle of bone and sinew stretch down over him. Her mouth fell open and a groan of despair arose from far inside her.

When they got onto the highway again, she said in an exhausted voice, "Just drive."

This was enough to set Joe on a kind of dream in which the details of the road, the steadily expanding immediate memories, the cornucopia of bright new prospects all flowed together in a sort of narcosis. Joe pictured, in an extremely vague setting, a kind of life with Ellen and Clara. There seemed to be a convenient flow of pavement from the interstate to their exit and from their exit to Ellen's street. Indeed, they were nearly to the house when she cried, "Stop!" in a voice so startling that Joe slammed on the brakes. "It's my husband," she said. Joe expected a sinking feeling but got none. He was actually excited to get a look at Billy again.

But then the car in front of Ellen's house pulled out.

"I guess we're safe," Joe said. "He's leaving."

"Follow him," said Ellen.

"Follow him?"

"You heard me."

This last seemed so peremptory that Joe started after the car, a Plymouth Valiant, in a very uncertain state. They went down past the city park and turned toward the river. They left the older, prim homes of the town and entered a district of split levels and unfinished wood, of newly sodded lawns with dark green seams where the strips met the day lawn arrived. Billy's car stopped and Joe stopped, perhaps a half block behind. Ellen was slumped to dash level.

"He's after that bitch again," she hissed. "And look how he's dressed!"

Billy Kelton threw his legs out, then unreeled himself from the car. He was still the striking-looking, lanky cowboy Joe remembered, and he looked as capable as ever of giving Joe a good thrashing. Joe couldn't see anything abnormal in the way he was dressed. He loped to the house. He had no chance to knock on the door: a slender arm thrust it open and he vanished without any change in his stride. Ellen unlatched the door to Joe's car.

"I've had it up to here," she said. "Can't thank you enough."

Ellen got out of the car, walked up in front of the house as forthright as a hostess and got into Billy's car. She started the engine and blew the horn. In a moment, Billy emerged from the house and walked over, eyes downcast. He lifted the straw hat from his head, wiped his forehead with his shirt sleeve, and replaced the hat. He stood by the car. He talked without raising his eyes. He rested the tips of his fingers on the side of the car and his eyes started to elevate. Some relief was in sight. He bent slightly and looked inside. He smiled suddenly. He leaned inside for a kiss. Then there was a bit of distress. Ellen had evidently rolled his head up in the electric window. The car pulled forward and Billy was dragged a few yards. Then the car stopped for more negotiation. He was dragged once more and released. Rubbing his neck and turning his head to one side, he walked around to the passenger's door and got in. As they drove away together, Joe watched the car intensely, certain that it would stop again, and Ellen would get out. But it just didn't happen. At least, Billy hadn't spotted him.

That night, Joe reflected on all this as he watched the Miss Universe contest. Miss Chile won. As the other contestants, in their terrible feigned happiness at her victory, covered Miss Chile with kisses, leaving red marks like wounds, her tiara was knocked askew. The camera caught the brief instant in which Miss Chile looked like a buffoon, a moment deftly corrected when Bob Barker rearranged the tiara with a self-deprecating shrug and grin, and with the nonchalance of one who adjusted ten thousand tiaras a day. It was late and Joe was tired.

Ralph of Ralph's Repair died. Joe couldn't exactly
remember him but evidently he'd repaired some things for
him in the past. Lureen called and said that she and Smitty
had legal business in Billings and would Joe be kind enough
to represent the family at the funeral. Ralph was cremated
and an old couple in almost matching light blue pantsuits came
out from Yakima for the jar. "Do you know those people?"
asked Mary Lynn Anderson, the piano teacher from Rapelje.
Mary Lynn had recently been dried out at the Rimrock Foun-
dation in Billings and she had this maddening energy, a real
born-again quality that was entirely trained on making up for
lost time. She wore a cotton checked shirt of pale green that
set off her tanned arms. She used to look religious when she
was drinking, spiritually enraptured, but dried out she looked
oversexed.

"Who are those people?" she asked Joe specifically, looking
at the old people.

"Some kind of connections of Ralph's," Joe said.

"His folks?"

"Beats me. Somebody told me when I came in that's who they were."

"I sent some flowers to the family. I wonder if they got there."

"I don't know."

"Well, I don't want to put them under pressure but I'd sure as heck like to know if my flowers ever got there. There was a note too."

The memorial service was being held at the little Carnegie library. Joe hadn't been to one of these since his Uncle Jerry was run over by a uranium truck. There were nine people there and five of them were browsing in the stacks. They had agreed to avoid a conventional service as being unsuited to Ralph's memory. The result was that nothing was happening. And in fact, Mildred Davis was trying to renew her library card and her husband Charlie was reading *Field and Stream*. Charlie was famous from opening up on his fourteen-year-old son with his fists for being in town without his cowboy hat on. Terry Smith had a Bible but he was completely furtive about it. Billy Kelton came in wearing his yellow slicker. He stared over at Joe, trying to remember him; Joe didn't help. Then Billy must have recalled their childhood differences, and he looked off in embarrassment. Joe still burned at those memories. Everyone went to the window to watch the new rain. "God, we needed that," said Alvie Skibstad, his gleaming white forehead contrasting with his dark face. "Take some of the fun out of it for the hoppers." Jim Carter came in the door soaked. He was only nineteen but his father had Alzheimer's and Jim had been running the ranch since he was fifteen; he bore the kind of weariness people rarely have at that age. "Headgate burst and run out over Main Street. The dry goods store is flooded." Charlie Davis looked up from *Field and*

Stream, and said, "It happens every year." "Naw, it don't," said Jim, tired of old-timers' bullshit, tired in general.

"I hope this doesn't sound disrespectful," said Mildred Davis, "but we're sure going to miss Ralph when things are broken." The only place she had been able to find to sit was behind the counter where the librarian usually sat. She wore a dark blue dress and a pillbox hat from which a piece of starchy lace projected, as though subtly indicating the prevailing wind. The old couple from Yakima looked around like a pair of immigrants.

"Nope," said Charlie. He licked the ends of the first two fingers of his right hand and began madly leafing through the magazine as though he'd left his social security card in there somewhere. "It doesn't sound disrespectful."

They all sat around vaguely, unmotivated; heads began to hang at odd angles. Nothing is an emergency around here, Joe thought, and I'm not so sure that's good.

"I wonder if we ought to say something about Ralph?" Joe asked. Billy was now staring at him. Nobody said anything. A couple of people looked like they might have wanted to but couldn't quite come up with the right idea. "Well," Joe said, "I don't mind saying a few words. For all these years, when we have had things broken, little things, important things, things which allowed our lives to flow, Ralph was there to set them spinning along again and with them, our lives too seemed repaired, whether it was a toaster, a television, a tractor, or a tire."

"You're thinking of Ralph's over to Lewistown," said Billy Kelton.

"I am?"

"Yeah, this one only did appliances."

"Well, I think appliances have become central to our lives," Joe said.

"Forget it."

A silence fell. Billy looked around. He caught the eyes of the connections from Yakima, and then addressed them. There was fire in his eyes.

"The Bible makes us the promise that our dead ones will live," he told them in a clear and direct voice. "They will rise up. 'The righteous themselves will possess the earth and they will reside forever upon it.' I don't know who exactly you are to Ralph but you may feel the lamentation of King David at the death of Absalom. And if so, we remind you that God did not originally intend for us to die. But because of the Adam and Eve business, he pretty much had to let us all return to dust as a payment for sin. But what we expect around these parts is that at the time of the Resurrection, Ralph's got a better than even chance of being called and that's about all you can ask. We knew him fairly well." It got pleasantly quiet as everyone took this in.

People began to leave. "I'll lock up," said Mildred Davis. Joe went out. For some reason, the smell of newly turned gardens along the street reminded him of the ocean and impressions came back of heat and rain, of docks steaming after a cloudburst. He thought of the repairs of Ralph. He couldn't quite seem to place Ralph. He guessed he had made that fairly clear. I've got to get out of this fog, Joe thought. He just couldn't believe he'd gotten the wrong fucking Ralph.

Dear Joe,

I am really enjoying pursuing our relationship through the U.S. Mail. Your letters are concise. There is the illusion of decision. The dime store Hamlet you so frequently seemed to be is nowhere in sight. Instead of the oscillating and confused so-called thinker, I have the image of a man struggling to hold on to family land, to lend his best efforts to the creation of vast beef herds. Joe, this ties you heart and soul to every hamburger stand in America. And I think you need that. I think it will humanize you to know your life depends on mob whimsy because your poetic detachment is enough to make me throw up. Maybe this will cause it to go away. Maybe arguing with normal people who want to do something different with your family place will help you see that there are other criteria in human relationships than whether or not people agree with you.

If by some remote chance, all of this has the effect of returning you to the human race, it would make me happy if we could see one another again.

Love,
Astrid

Joe let this soak; then, to heat it up, he wrote back a few days later. As he wrote the letter, he felt an inexplicable, mad, tingling ache.

Dear Astrid,

Your letter seems to take the position that it is in reply to a letter from me. I have not written you. But it is nice to have yours anyway. As for here, it is not so bad. I am leading a baffling life but I am suited to that. I have barely had a chance to look into the sort of shooting we may expect this fall; and in fact all the little pleasures have gone by the way, not because I am so busy but because I am apathetic from being unable to completely understand what I am doing all this for. I wonder if you remember the great number of mountain hippies we used to have around here. Well, they are all running tax shelters for environmentalist organizations and I plan to meet with a few to see if we can save a buck or two as well as take the fun out of breaking this thing up for my greedy connections. Why haven't they moved away? I have found on my return that going out to seek your fortune no longer has the prestige it once had. Now on return they give you that fishy look and ask, "Back for the summer?" This proves to me that it is the rats who *do* stick with a sinking ship. No reference to you of course darling. I have had numerous opportunities to confirm that in fact I trust nobody. Which has its distorting effect. But we all live beneath some sort of lens and no true shapes can be discerned. I think it is quite enough to be able to tell someone what is on your mind, even if the delivery is nervous and sidelong. Therefore, this letter, my ideal recipient. — Still not getting any. How about yourself?

Joe signed it "With suspicious affection," licked the envelope, and threw it on the kitchen counter for the next trip to town. But before he could get it into the mail, he received yet another letter from Astrid, a short one. It said, "I hate you. You stole my car. Now I hate all men." He fired back one more.

Dear Astrid,
    God made women because sheep can't cook.
Joe

He sent this latest with a gleeful and almost breathless air, reflected in the enormous cost of sending it by overnight mail. He must have known that it would have a big effect. He must have planned this bit of explosive infantilism without a hint of innocence. Because in four days flat Astrid, wearing enormous dark glasses, dragging more luggage than she looked like she had the strength to carry, walked in the front door and said, "Take it back, motherfucker."

He was so happy! He loved her with his whole heart. And then tears came into his eyes.

"Met anyone nice out here?" Astrid asked.

"One. But I already knew her, really."

"Get anywhere?"

"I would."

"Only what?"

"I keep laughing at the wrong time."

"I *see*."

He couldn't fathom her. It was like Jackie O at the funeral

of Onassis. One suspected the sunglasses concealed twinkling eyes. When Astrid wished to tell him something important, she would grab his forearm the way children do to each other in the scary parts of movies. She did that now. "Do try to remember the week we had," she said. "All those funny things that weren't funny."

"Like what wasn't funny?"

"Farting in time to music."

"What else?"

"Calling me drunk at three a.m. and shouting, 'Don't pay the ransom, I've escaped!' Joe, you were a hoot!"

A certain formality was agreed upon without discussion: Astrid would have her own room. As it happened, the two bedrooms were on opposite sides of the kitchen and so the sense of division was fairly complete. It was Joe's plan to make this arrangement clear to Ellen as soon as he could. He didn't think that that was absolutely required; and in fact he meant to be sure his explanation did not imply a deeper responsibility to Ellen than necessary. He just wanted it clear. Astrid settled right into the arrangement without particularly indicating whether she was there for a day or a year. Joe didn't plan to ask. He didn't mention his daughter because he wanted to make certain a reasonable plan for visiting was in place before he got down to the specifics of an arrangement.

He was immediately fascinated by Astrid's city ways, which he hadn't even noticed before. She folded her things in her dresser and hung her blouses carefully in the closet. She got a glass from the kitchen to put in the bathroom cabinet and set a bottle of French perfume on the dresser where the brassieres were folded one cup inside the other. She tied the curtains in their middles to let in light, stretched the bedspread taut and placed a travel-battered paperback next to the bed.

Joe noticed all this as breezily as he could, but since he had no real routines in this house, no routines anywhere really, it was hard to make a single natural movement at the same time he was observing Astrid. He simply felt her presence swelling and seeping throughout the house and found himself less and less able to even act as if he was ignoring it.

As they passed in the short corridor, he reached his hand out to her arm. She stopped at exactly that distance and said, "Yes?"

"Hi," he said, smiling, and feeling shockingly stupid.

She said, "Hi."

They passed going in opposite directions. Joe thought that to keep this business from degenerating at a very rapid rate, he was going to have to have something to do other than absorb the impact of Astrid.

He turned back from the living room and stretching his arms across the doorway, spoke down the corridor toward Astrid's room. "I'm going to run in and get a few supplies before things close."

"Bye," she called, "use your seat belt."

He sped to Ellen's bearing some peculiar force because she simply let him rush into her house and make love to her, bracing her pelvis while she scrutinized this demented, ejaculating person. Joe felt withered by her quizzical stare. He dressed so quickly afterward he had to pry himself back into his shorts. "I have to talk to you," he said, underlining this vagary with a powerful, fixed look. "You know what it's about. I feel I'm being strung along."

Ellen said, "You've got a lot of nerve after what we've just done."

"I mean, is this it? We're just going to sneak around like this?"

"It depends," Ellen said.

"Depends? On what?"

"On how I feel. God, Joe, you never changed! Can't you take one day at a time?"

"No," Joe said so loud it was almost a shout. *"I want to see my daughter!"*

He went to the IGA store and threw things arbitrarily into the shopping cart. He got stuck in the only check-out line that was open. A small, heavy woman in front of him, with a dirty-faced infant riding the cart, unloaded small items piled as high as her head. He stared at the front page of the *Star*, at the headline RABBIT FACE BABY HAS TEN INCH EARS, and read as much as he could of the text before he had to check out with his items: the dieting mother had binged on carrots during her final trimester.

As he unloaded his groceries in the kitchen, Astrid glided past him and said, "I smell what you've been doing."

He slowly turned in her direction, the burn of deep conviction; he was a bit too slow: she was already back in her room.

"When are you turning in that rental car?" he asked loudly.

"As soon as I can get to the airport," she said. "You can follow me."

"Why would I follow you?"

"So you can fucking well give me back my car."

Joe had once gone out with a girl who was just breaking up with her live-in boyfriend. He had quite fallen for this girl and had already begun worrying about the depth of his involvement. The boyfriend had recently moved out but he stopped back from time to time to bicker with the girl about the ownership of the stereo and the health of the bamboo plant he claimed to have nurtured to its current size, and to laugh sarcastically at the clean house she was currently keeping. As Joe watched the progress of these small nagging encounters, he began to suspect he was witnessing a preview of his own life. Detachment set in. Now, years later, he placed similar hopes on the pink car. Some nagging, the exchange of a few receipts, some appropriate body language, whirling departures or loud footsteps on the wooden floors of the ranch, and the slave chains could be gently lifted.

A few days later, he set up his drawing equipment in the kitchen, where the light was good and the coffee was close. But he knew it was a lie and he put it all away again. It was as if he was posing these materials. Astrid came in wearing her wrapper drawn close around her with one hand and carrying a cup and saucer in the other. She went to the sink and looked out the window. Joe felt that there was something brewing: the set of her mouth, her silence, something. He managed to watch her without being intrusive. As she looked through the kitchen window, her expression began to fill, to bloom, and he knew an emotion was cresting, an exclamation was at hand.

"Get a load of that ghastly dog!" she screeched. Joe jumped.

"Is he out there?" Joe got up and went to the window. The dog, lightly blurred with new fur, sidled over the lawn, glancing at the house, his corkscrew tail shifting metronomically over his back.

"I never saw one quite like that," said Astrid.

"I can't believe he's just out walking around."

"He's like something from outer space," she said. "I want to go see him."

"He'll be back under the house the second he sees you."

Joe watched from the kitchen window. He saw the dog react to the motion of the inside kitchen door. His tail sagged to the horizontal. His lower jaw dropped slightly and his ears clenched into a suspicious knot on top of his head. Then Astrid appeared in the picture. She said something to the dog. She patted the tops of her knees. The crown of the dog's head smoothed as his ears dropped adorably. He bounced back and forth, then bounded to Astrid and licked her face. She found a stick for him to fetch; but when she reared back to throw it, he yelped and ran under the house. Astrid went over and lay on her stomach to plead with the dog. Joe wound open the kitchen window and hauling himself forward over the sink and faucets was able to look straight down on the lower half of Astrid's torso; the rest of her was under the house. She had let the wrapper slip up so that the hard shape of her buttocks was visible up to where they were sliced from view by the clapboard siding. "Aw, come on," she was saying, "whaddya say?" Joe's face was only a matter of feet from her bare loins and he could feel himself swelling abruptly against the sink. Astrid began to back out from under the house. He was terrified that she would discover him hanging out of the kitchen window, and he grappled his way inside, managing to hit one of the faucets in his rush, and soaking the front of his pants. By the time he was standing flatfooted on the kitchen floor once more, Astrid walked back in, stared at his wet bulging crotch, and said, "What have you been doing" in an uninflected voice. It was not a question. She sighed deeply and went into her room.

"Let me see if we can't just drop the rental car right in town," he said into the bedroom doorway.

"Give her my regards," said Astrid, in a kind of trill.

"You can reach me at my aunt and uncle's," he called back. "The number's by the phone." He paused in the doorway, soundless, in case anything could be heard from her direction, any little thing. But it was quiet.

He shot into Smitty and Lureen's. He didn't really want to stop, hadn't intended to. As soon as he got there, he called the ranch. "It occurred to me," he said to Astrid, "that the number might actually *not* be there—"

"It is."

"Okay," he sang, "that's all I had in mind."

"Bye."

Smitty was alone. Lureen had gone to do something at the rectory. Smitty sat at the kitchen table, his hands clasped on its top. He wore the familiar suit pants and his shirt was buttoned right up to his throat. He seemed to stand before some final and invisible inquisition as he wailed, "Here I am living on leftover chicken salad and baked beans! While Lureen dusts for that double-chinned preacher!"

It might have been his present mood or his recollection of his gingerly first night here, but Joe said, "Then why don't you get up off your ass and cook something?"

After a long moment, Smitty said, "I have decided that I didn't hear you. You have still got, by special dispensation, an unblemished record in this house."

"I just wanted to check in and see if you and Lureen are getting along okay."

"We are, if you think so. We're not complaining. The Overstreets are not happy about you running those cattle. I don't know what we, or at least Lureen, are going to live on."

"I think you're going to be fine," said Joe and went out.

"You forgot your thesaurus!" Smitty called from the stoop.

"I'll be back!" Standing in front of the two-story blue expanse of clapboard in the perfectly centered doorway, Smitty reminded Joe of a cuckoo clock. Smitty used to be a man about town, but there were only one or two apertures in the building in which he appeared now: the front door and his bedroom window.

Joe drove down Benteen Street and turned on Fifth, went a couple of blocks in an old neighborhood whose telephone wires came through heavy foliage and slumped low over the street. Plastic three-wheelers were parked on the sidewalk. A woman smoked and seriously watched her dachshund move along the band of grass between the sidewalk and the street. Another woman stood in the street and waved her husband on as he backed his Buick slowly from an old garage. At a certain point, she flattened her palms in his direction, the car stopped, she got in, and they drove off. There was a five-cent lemonade sign but no stand. Finally, with a flourish, Joe arced Astrid's rental car into Ellen's driveway. As soon as he had stopped, the engine still running, the passenger door opened and Billy Kelton climbed in.

"Hi, Billy."

"Let's take a ride," he said.

Joe put the car in reverse. "Any spot in particular?"

"You pick."

Joe crossed the neighborhood the way he had come. He made a point of greeting people with a small neighborly wave. Most responded as from long acquaintanceship except the lady with the dachshund, who was sufficiently possessed to remove her cigarette and squint after him with irritation. Billy exhibited a lazy athletic grace. He was dressed more conventionally now in a pair of Wranglers and a blue work shirt. He had a hardbitten, thin-lipped, fairly handsome face, and a husky voice.

"I don't know what to do about the fact you've been seeing Ellen . . ."

Joe looked out to the oncoming street. He set his head to one side as though about to speak. Then nothing came.

"I fought for a country I'm not sure I care to live in. But while I'm here I can find a few ways to make it my own. If you follow me."

"Not completely. And I thought your marriage was on the rocks. Weren't you seeing someone just the other day? But yes, Billy, I missed the war in Vietnam."

"Well, there you go. That's about it, isn't it."

Joe could nearly feel the heat of his stare. They drove on down past the wool docks alongside the railroad tracks and then curved on up toward the courthouse.

"I don't want to just go to spelling things out here, pardner, but there's this little country of my own where I make all the laws. Do you believe me?"

Joe pulled up in front of the glass doors of the sheriff's office. They could look through the windshield, through the door, and see law officers. It would be an easy thing to honk on the horn. Joe tapped it lightly; two officers glanced out and he waved them off as though he had bumped the horn accidentally.

"Why wouldn't I believe you?" Joe said bitterly. "If you'll admit being in that war you've got nothing to hide. Now, do you want to walk, or shall I? I don't care, this is a rental car anyway."

"I'll walk, thanks. But just take me pretty serious here. It's important. Ellen and I haven't given up. And we have a sweet little girl that's worth any sacrifice we might make."

20

"And B," said Astrid, "it's time you potty-trained your mind. Especially as relates to me and my activities."

He didn't dare ask what A was. She was drinking and had *been* drinking. Nevertheless, she looked quite attractive with her dark hair still wet from the shower, its ends soaking the light blue dress at its shoulders. It was very rare for Astrid to drink too much. This was just fascinating. Everything she did fascinated Joe.

"I don't know much about your activities," said Joe coldly.

"Did you see the little chiquita?" Astrid inquired. Joe couldn't understand why in this age women in the throes of jealousy always used these ghastly diminutives on one another. The chiquita, the cutie, the little woman, the wifette.

"You know, I missed her. Isn't that a shame?"

"I think it is a shame," Astrid wailed, "that you can't have everything you want every minute of the day. You once employed all your arty bullshit to make me feel that I fulfilled something in you."

"We grow."

"You grow. I don't."

"Careful now. We want to avoid the emetic side of boozy self-pity."

She gave him the finger with one hand and raised her glass to her lips with the other. "Joe Blow," she said with a smile, "the man in translation."

"My God! We throw nothing away! We never know when we might need it!"

"You lost that round, dopey. Go make some dinner. My stomach thinks my throat's been cut, or whatever they say out here."

At first he didn't think he would cook, because she suggested it. He then decided that that in itself indicated lack of independence and went to the kitchen to begin. As he cooked, he watched to see if she would make herself another drink. She didn't. She watched the news (excitement about medium-range missiles). She was looking out into the world. He was looking into the sink. It had just gotten real slow. The terrible slowness was coming over him. He lifted his face to the doorway and there she was, fast-forwarding world news facts into her skull with the television. It didn't seem to matter that she was drunk; it wouldn't make any real difference. It wouldn't turn medium-range missiles into long-range missiles. It wouldn't sober her up unless the actual TV blew up in her actual face.

"What are you cooking?" she called.

"Couple of omelets. Not too much stuff in the fridge."

"No rat poison, please!"

He chopped up some bell peppers and crookneck squash and scallions. He made everything astonishingly uniform. While he beat the eggs, Astrid came in and refilled her drink. She watched him cook. As he heated the skillet, she said, "No, you don't want sex with me just now. You were too busy jacking off while I tried to make friends with your dog." She went back into the living room and fell into her chair. Joe overcame his inertia and finished cooking. He finally got things on the kitchen table and called Astrid. She came and sat down. "I have just seen something very interesting on television," she said, avidly eating her omelet. "This is good."

"What did you see?"

"A report on grizzly bear attacks. It's so exciting here in Montana! The victims tend to be menstruating women!"

"That's not so hard to understand."

"Ha ha ha. He tips his hand."

"I didn't mean it as a joke," he said.

He couldn't eat. His omelet was a folded yellow fright. His hands were sweating. The glare on the kitchen windows was such that you wouldn't necessarily know if someone was looking in. A shining drop of water hung on the faucet without falling.

"Here's my exit," she intoned. "I get my period. I go hiking in Glacier National Park."

"Let's hope it doesn't come to that."

She started laughing hard and loud. She stopped. Her chin dropped to her chest. A guffaw burst through her nose. She covered her mouth and twisted her face off to one side. "I'm so sorry—" She threw up on the kitchen floor.

"That's enough for me," said Joe and got to his feet.

"Don't put any more miles on that rent-a-car," she shouted as he went out the door. Immediately, he could hear her crying.

"The things alcohol makes us do," he thought, walking across the yard. "Leading cause of hospitalization, leading cause of incarceration"—he began marching to this meter—

"leading cause of broken families, leading cause of absentee-ism, leading cause of half-masters, leading cause of fascination with inappropriate orifices, leading cause of tooth decay, leading cause of communism, leading cause of Christian fundamentalism, leading cause of hair loss, leading cause of dry loins, leading cause of ulcerated chickens, leading cause of styrofoam. Ah, mother and father," he wheezed, out of breath. "Time to arise. Time to buck some bales up onto the stack." Moonlight dropped upon him. He walked out into the prairie whose humming had stopped at sundown. A fall of frost had begun and the grassy hummocks were starred with ice. The gleam of canine eyes caught the moonlight.

21

Joe spent the following day with the state brand inspector, trying to organize all his cattle receipts. When he got home, Astrid was in bed. She was running a high fever and had sunk into a glumly witty state of disassociated illness. She looked so helpless, so dependent, so unlike anything he'd ever seen before in Astrid that he felt an abounding sweetness well up within. He was sorry that it seemed so inappropriate to mention his declining fortunes. He was under a momentary spell of amicability. People at full strength were better able to sustain their loathing, and avoid these vague and undrained states.

"My darling," said Joe.

"Do you know who's been just swell?" she asked, propping herself up in bed. She looked like a pretty nun without makeup and with her hair pulled back.

"Who?"

"Smitty."

"Smitty? How do you know Smitty?"

"He's been by. And I mean swell."

"That's quite strange."

"He seems so concerned! He's concerned with everything. He just trains this concern on things. What concern is shown by Smitty!"

"What about Lureen? She been by?"

"She was here too. Now that one isn't sure about me. But Smitty is so lovely. He thought he might be able to get me some insurance."

"You didn't go for it, did you?"

"No, but I gave him fifty bucks for some kind of filing fee."

"I know that filing fee. It's called Old Mr. Boston Dry Gin."

"I couldn't say. I went for his story. It charmed me. I'm already bored. I wish I was back in Florida, fucking and using drugs. It's easy to grow nostalgic in a situation like this."

"Oh, darling, just stop," he said, annoyed by his own reaction. He thought of vigorous, robust Ellen, ranch girl, heartening the next generation with teaching. Difficult to imagine her saying in the middle of lovemaking, as Astrid once did, "Now I'd like it up my ass." He had prevaricated, he recalled, then ultimately brooded about the prospects of a second chance.

"You know it's funny," said Joe, wondering why he didn't appreciate Astrid any more than he did. "I've had such a thing for this schoolteacher."

"Do I have to hear this?"

"I'm trying to keep you entertained. We're beyond any little ill feelings along these lines anyway, aren't we? Besides if I tell you this in a sarcastic way and make it good and trivial I can write 'finis' to the sonofabitch." It wasn't true. He wanted to hurt her. He was laying in stores to hate himself.

"Knock yourself out. I really don't care."

Joe believed her. There was malice in his continuation of

145

the story. It was temporarily beyond him to take stock of the gravity of their situation. It was an awful moment.

"Anyway, I've been drawn to her innocence, whether or not it exists. It may not exist. But I took it as a working proposition that the innocence was real."

"Did you stick it in?"

"I'm afraid I did."

"She can't be that innocent."

"But we had these wonderful little skits. I knew her years ago. We hit golf balls together. We discussed her background on the ranch."

"You stuck it in."

"We stuck it in. We had meals together in an atmosphere that combined lightheartedness and high courtship. We went for a long drive."

"This is to puke over," said Astrid.

"Now, Astrid. There was something quite delicate. A picture had begun to form." Joe felt like a vampire.

"I can see that picture."

"But wait. I had decided to marry her. We would live together in the picture that had begun to form. I flew to New York and quit my job with Ivan. I was exhausted. When I was flying home, the country unfolded beneath the wings and it all came to me that—I don't like that smile, Astrid—I would marry this lovely girl. And I must say, that is a very nasty smile, indeed."

"I shouldn't laugh," said Astrid. "I am in the dreary mental situation in which sneezing, laughing, coughing, calling the dog, or ensemble singing are equally uncomfortable. Anyway, what happened is that you thought it over and upon consideration, upon the most serious consideration you—"

"No. Not this time. I called and before I had the chance to

propose, her husband went for a ride with me and told me that they were working it out."

"There's a husband?"

"And a right odd one at that. He used to thrash me when I was a boy, beat me like a gong."

"Well, if you'd had any conviction, you'd have argued with him. If you'd had the kind of conviction that it would take to go back to your painting, you'd have told that hubby off. Now what've you got? A trashy-mouth Cuban who doesn't appreciate you."

"Oh, darling," said Joe in a flat and uninterested tone, "don't be so hard on yourself."

Astrid's weeping was real. Joe could scarcely remonstrate with her. She had every right to this. His position had eroded and he could not say a thing. Instead, he gazed through the window at nothing and came to appreciate how wonderful much of the world could seem.

Collecting herself, she said, "Well, what am I to do?"

"I'm not good at this," said Joe.

Astrid tried to shift her weight slightly. She sighed. "Given my desperation, I wonder if you'd have time to murmur some smut in my ear."

"Astrid."

"Something about the schoolteacher possibly. Anything. There was a fly in the room earlier. You can't imagine my absorption in watching its confused circuit of my room."

"I hope you're resisting ideas like that."

"What easy ideas have you resisted?"

"I hate you."

"I hate you too."

The sudden bitterness of these remarks was stunning. Literally, they were both stunned by what they had said. They had heard it before and it was still utterly stunning, as stunning to hear as to say.

He rose to go. "We don't mean that."

"We don't?" said Astrid. She looked exhausted. He was horribly sorry that he hadn't headed the moment off. But they had been in this intense snare for so long. It was hard to keep things from just running their course.

22

The next day Lureen was on the phone at seven.

"Joe, I don't know if you realize this but Smitty has been bringing seafood up from Texas in a refrigerated truck. I mean, he's brokering it, not physically doing it himself, and he has run into a hitch."

"Which is?" Joe asked, knowing that he had just learned where the lease money had gone, some of it anyway.

"I hear your suspicion already. Now, I want you to give this a fair hearing."

"Sock it to me, Lureen."

"Well, a big load of it spoiled."

"That's a shame. I'm sorry to hear it."

"But it was insured."

"When did this happen?"

"Three weeks ago."

"How much was it insured for?"

"Thirty thousand."

"Wow, that's a powerful load of shrimp. Did he collect?"

"Not yet. But I'm sure he will."

"So what's the problem?"

"The problem is that the insurance company has initiated an investigation. They want to actually *view* the spoiled shrimp. Smitty said, It's a little late now, I buried it. And the investigators said, We want to see the spot. So, Smitty very graciously took them out to the place—"

"Wait a minute. Where?"

"*There*. You were in New York. And up by the burn pit, he showed them the empty boxes, but they wanted to see the shrimp. Smitty couldn't believe his ears. The what? he said. And real rudelike, the chief investigator says, *The shrimp, the shrimp, the shrimp!* It's been three weeks! Smitty told him. They have decomposed! You got it? But—and it's a big 'but'—this horrible man, this investigator said, Nope, there'd still be shells. I don't know where this all leads but, Joe, for my own peace of mind, I know you've spent time down in the Florida—"

"Right, Lureen, I've seen a world of shrimp."

"Would there still be, after all these weeks, any indication —I won't say *evidence*—that there had been any shrimp?"

"Yes. Shells. Tens of thousands of them, by the sound of it."

"Joe, we've tried so hard to be nice to you and make you feel to home . . ."

It was too late. She had already signed for the cattle. Joe put the receiver down slowly and carefully. At first, he was contrite: he could have said something more reassuring. But, like what? He was entirely limited to exaggerating the speed at which shrimp shells decompose. How else could he explain Lureen's belligerence? Surely she was not one hundred percent taken in by Smitty, the bounder. She must know he meant to glom the ranch, mustn't she?

Joe actually saw Smitty drive up. Smitty wasn't going very fast when he came in the driveway, but he stabbed the brakes so that the blue and white Ford skidded a little on the gravel. He sort of threw himself from the car, flinging the door shut behind him. At first, he seemed in a hurry but he lost a little speed by the time he actually got to the front door.

"Smitty," said Joe, opening the door for him. He reached out his hand. Smitty gave it a glance before shaking it.

"Have you got a minute?"

"Sure I do, Smitty. Coffee?"

"No, I'm fine. Where can we sit?"

They went into the living room. Smitty glanced around at the books, the family pictures, the braided riata that hung on a hook by the door, the college diplomas, the brands burned into the wood, the chunks of quartz that old settler had mortared into the fireplace. They sat down.

"What's the deal, Joe?"

"Sir?"

"The deal. What are you doing back here?"

"Well, I just wanted to come back."

"You did."

"And I thought, somewhere along the way, we might do more with the place. The spotted knapweed and spurge are kind of taking over. Russian thistle. The fellows who lease it don't care about the old ranch. Fences falling. Springs gone."

"Leasing is the only money there is left in these places."

"The money? What money? So far as I can tell, the grazing fees aren't even making it to Lureen."

"We're listing it as a receivable. We've had some problem collecting. If we can't collect it, we can write it off. We all need that."

"To write it off you're going to have to sue the man that owes it to you. The government requires that."

"Whatever."

"Maybe the rancher you were dealing with needed to be examined more closely."

"He's over twenty-one. What can I say?"

Smitty put a cigarette in the exact center of his mouth and with a book of matches in his hands, rested his elbows on his knees, looked off into space and thought. "Joe," he said and lit the cigarette. "Why don't you kiss my ass?"

"Because I have preserved my options, Smitty. One of them is to keep an eye on you." Then he added, "I know the seafood business hasn't treated you well. You must be under pressure." Smitty's eyes flicked off to the wall.

Well, thought Joe, at least it's a beginning; we'll gradually move old Smitty into position and then do the right thing. He watched Smitty and tried to get to the bottom of the combined helplessness and guile, without much luck. The signals of an old boozer like Smitty, thrown off by the cheesy deliquescence of the brain itself, were seldom instructive.

The glow of Astrid's cigarette in the twilight of her room looked as cheerful as a Cub Scout campfire to Joe as he finished telling her the whole story. He leaned over from his straightback metal chair and lifted the cigarette from her lips. He hadn't had a cigarette in almost a month. He was tempted to take a drag and told Astrid so. "Don't," she said. "It's so hard to quit." He could feel her easy thought. "God," she said, "that's a wonderful story. But you must have such complicated feelings about all this."

"I'm working on it."

Astrid began laughing. She was really laughing too hard. He leaned over and gripped her shoulders to steady her. The laughter made him nervous and he took her cigarette. He had to stick her cigarette way out in the corner of his own mouth to keep the smoke out of his eyes. Then her face began to glisten with tears. Anyway, she wasn't laughing anymore. Joe sat off to one side, holding her cigarette for her.

"One of these days," he said, "it's going to get cold. And that beautiful white snow is going to come floating down."

Joe arranged to buy an old iron woodstove from a rancher up toward the Musselshell River. It was in one of the livestock papers and he bought it very inexpensively, but he had to haul it himself. He took the flatbed truck and drove up through a vast expanse of bluish sage-covered hills. He went through two isolated hamlets, huddled with their Snow Cats and hay sleds piled outside in the heat. One little town had a bar the size of a single-car garage and a log post office that seemed dwarfed by its wind-whipped flag. He drove up to the edge of a stand of lodgepole pines bordered by a big buffalo grass pasture. Someone was burning ditches and high above the column of smoke a blue heron soared, trailing its legs, looking for its accustomed lowlands. Old black automobile tires hung on the fenceposts, painted *Keep Out* as a small log house was approached. The house sat low and defensive behind a field of discarded machinery: old iron wheels, wooden spokes, and last year's winter kill dragged out among the disarray—hides over skeletons, decomposing calves.

An old man answered the door, a glass of whiskey in one hand, his stomach hanging over the top of his pants and chew dribbling out the corners of his mouth. He had hairy nostrils and small, crinkled eyes. "Here for the stove?"

"Yeah, I am." Joe got the money out of his shirt and reached it to him.

"Thank you much," said the old man.

"There's a Farmhand on the Minneapolis-Moline. You load that thing on your own?"

"You bet."

The old man narrowed the doorway. He scrutinized Joe. "Sonny Starling wouldn't be your daddy, would he?"

"Yes, sir, that he was," Joe said. The old man nodded and thought.

"He was a hand, really what you'd call a pretty hand."

"That's what I've heard," said Joe.

"But the bank took all the pretty out of your old man."

"Yes, sir."

"He come in and ruint me in 'fifty-six. I never made her back. That bank just took Sonny and made him into an entirely different feller."

Joe had heard this sort of thing before.

"Well, let me get loaded out of here," he said.

"That's a hell of a way to get ahead in the world."

"Maybe," said Joe, "but anyway, he's dead."

"Good," said the old man.

Joe threw himself into loading the stove. He lowered it onto the flatbed with the Farmhand and boomed it down with some chain he had brought along for the purpose. Evidently the old man didn't need it anymore. He had a better one or he'd gone to electric or gas. Joe started back. When he was nearly home, he saw a pickup truck pulled off the interstate next to the barbed wire. A man stood next to a horse whose head hung close to the ground. The man looked quite helpless and Joe sensed the horse was at the end of the line. It was at this point that his eyes finally filled with tears.

23

Joe drove to Billings on Tuesday to meet with an attorney for the Continental Divide Insurance Company. He dressed in a coat and tie and parked the old flatbed far enough away to dissolve association with it by the time he reached the office. He was early.

He walked into the Hart-Albin store to use up a few minutes and collect his thoughts. He strolled through the toiletries section, admiring the beautiful young women who sold perfumes and intimate soaps, and who tried the delicate atomizers on one another. He sprayed some sample cologne on himself. The glass display cases revealed an Arabic world of indulgence. He tried more cologne. He invented biographies for the salesladies. Reared on hog farms or in the families of railroad mechanics, each greeted her discovery by the perfume manager with an effulgent blossoming. He politely tested one last cologne with a sweaty squeeze of the bulb. A musky, faraway penumbra engulfed him, quite startling in its power.

Time to go to the lawyer. He crossed the street, walked half a block north, and entered the offices. He announced himself to the secretary and immediately the lawyer, Gene Bowen, appeared at his door and gestured Joe inside with a handful of papers. Bowen was a lean, harried-looking man, plainly bright and short of time.

Bowen moved around behind his desk. Joe sat in a comfortable chair in front of it. Bowen rested his chin on his hands and let Joe begin. "My Uncle Smitty, Smith Starling—"

"Yes," said Bowen decisively, suddenly wrinkling his nose. Joe was astonished at the lawyer's reaction to the mention of Smitty's name. "Is that you? What is that?" Then Joe understood Bowen's reaction.

"Canoe."

"You what?"

"Canoe. It's a cologne. And a couple of others. Musk was one."

"Very well. Go ahead. Didn't mean to interrupt."

"My Uncle Smitty—"

"Would you be offended if I opened a window?"

"Not at all."

Bowen got up and struggled with the window behind his desk without freeing it. "I'm gonna end up with a fucking hernia—"

"Here, let me help."

They got on either side of the window and heaved upward as hard as they could. Bowen pulled his face to one side and wrinkled his nose fiercely. "It's not as if it was some kind of animal droppings," Joe said.

The bottom of the window casement tore free; wood fragments and dried putty flew across Bowen's desk. His finger was bleeding. He walked around and opened his door. "Let that air out while I get a Band-Aid."

The secretary poked her head in. "What's going on in here?"

"We had a little trouble with the window."

"I'd better ring up maintenance." Turning to Joe, she asked, "May I ask what you're wearing?"

Joe was getting angry. "I mixed a few scents, trying them out. But socially speaking, I've had better luck shitting my pants."

Bowen returned and went straight to his desk. "Leave that open, Mildred," he said to the secretary, pointing at the door. "Let's try to bear down and get through this as fast as we can. Okay, 'Smitty' is your uncle. Smitty's got his tail in a crack. You want to help Smitty. Why?"

"I have an aunt who I like very much. She depends on him. They are like a little couple."

"They are."

"Yes."

"And what does she do?"

"She is a retired schoolteacher."

"So, she has a pension?"

"A small one, and a small income from a small family ranch."

"Which belongs to?"

"Uh, to Lureen. To my aunt."

"And Mister Smitty got his stake in the shrimp business by?"

"Mortgaging the ranch."

Bowen sucked on a paper clip pensively.

"It's none of my business, Mr. Starling. But why don't you let this wonderful fellow just go to jail?"

"I'm pursuing my aunt's interests, as I see them, as best I can."

"Okay," said Bowen, dropping his hands to the desk decisively. "I sense that we can speak to one another with candor."

"I sense the same," said Joe earnestly.

"May I be very direct with you?"

"Please."

"Joe, your aftershave stinks to high heaven."

"I really can't do anything about that now."

"As to Mister Smitty, yes, we can try to get the charges dropped. Yes, I foresee that being a discussable possibility. Under this scenario, Smitty fails to recoup the thirty thousand. *In addition to which*, the insurance company is out of pocket, I am guessing, another thirty, in fees, and in ascribable overhead."

"What overhead?"

"They've got twelve floors in Denver."

"I see. Well, look, let's examine the cost of dropping this. You get me some specifics and I'll try to sell it to my uncle."

"But remember, he doesn't have to buy it," said Bowen. "He can go to jail."

"I admit it's tempting," said Joe.

"The first time he stoops for the Lifebuoy in those big showers, he's going to meet some very nice Indians."

"Like I say," said Joe, "the temptation is there."

24

It was a long drive back. He listened to a local radio station for a while and absorbed himself in the community announcements. Money was being taken up to purchase bibs for senior citizens. A truculent Boy Scout made the following statement: "This week we decided what badges we are going to do. The two main ones are Tending Toddlers and Science-In-Action. And we are going to bring dues of twenty-five cents even if we are sick." After that a member of the Lions Club explained the problems they had had building a concession stand for Little League games. They had to find out if the neighbors would object. Zoning ordinances required it be a certain distance from the street. That meant they had to move the backstop. A building permit would have to be applied for. To meet Class A Residential zoning requirements, the concession stand would have to go between the pitcher's mound and first base. The planning board granted a special-use permit. So, after five years, they were now prepared to build the concession stand. Finally, before Joe shut the radio off, the fire chief said they were sick of putting out prairie fires started by the railroad.

Oh, this is an odd little life, he thought, turning onto Smitty and Lureen's street. Great shafts of sunlight came down between the old trees that lined the badly cracked sidewalk. A newspaper boy jumped the curb with his bicycle and a man in a wheelchair, wearing a tam-o'-shanter and smoking a cigar, coasted down the slight incline of the sidewalk serenely, the spokes of his wheels sparkling in the afternoon sun. Two young carpenters with a long plank resting on their shoulders, made a wide turn at the corner and disappeared. Pigeons poured out of the abandoned Methodist church like smoke and ascended into the sky; they were the reincarnated souls of miners, railroaders, and ranch hands. Things seemed so right to Joe, he was able to enfold himself in the breaking wave. Ambiguity was at a safe distance now; it was not necessary to have an opinion about anything.

Lureen led Joe into the parlor. She set out tea. He cast his eye over the curios and the lugubrious draperies that declared this an inner world. He felt he had arrived.

"I've been to see the lawyer for the insurance company."

"Oh," said Lureen, "I wonder if that was a good idea."

"I think it was. We talked about the possibility of dropping the charges."

"Let them charge him. He's innocent. They can take it to court. I almost prefer it. It's in the rumor mill anyway. It might be good to have Smitty's name cleared publicly."

"Are you certain this is your wish?"

"My wish is that it had never happened. But since it has, it has to be cleared. You know, I blame my own mother for this. She doted on me and I'm grateful for that. But to her dying day, she went around town saying, 'My daughter is an angel from heaven, but my two boys' — Smitty and your father — 'are common swindlers!' Words like this from a mother hang on in a small town for years."

Looking at Lureen as she poured the tea and thinking of the multitude of first- and second-graders who had gone on from her bare schoolroom greatly strengthened by her attentions, he couldn't help thinking his grandmother had been partly, and maybe entirely, right.

He was so fond of Lureen that, against his own inclinations, he said, "If you change your mind and I can help, let me know."

Lureen looked off and thought for a moment. "When you were a little boy, you sucked your thumb. You sucked your thumb until you were seven years old. And the orthodontist said it had given you a severe overbite and that if you didn't quit immediately, it would have to be corrected by surgery. Remember? It was in August and you were such a desperate little boy. But it was Smitty who sat up with you at night when you cried and put a sock over your hand and stayed up night after night with you — for a week! — until you succeeded. Night after night! He never had a drink until you quit. These people who want to put him in jail don't know anything about that side of Smitty."

Motoring along, unable to sort out his feelings about his aunt and uncle, he mused about his early days with Astrid — the high flying, the courtship, the glands titrating explosive juices into their systems, followed one noon by Astrid's announcement that she was considering suicide.

Later, she rejected it, saying, "Suicide is far too peculiar for me. It's something that should be done by science majors or Mormons. It should be done by people we know little about, like ship brokers and risk arbitragers."

They were so chipper then, embedded in time. Joe could paint blindfolded. They moved in the direction of their intentions as quickly as figures in cartoons. He remembered thinking it was swell past measuring. But somehow it got less juicy. Somehow it got annoying. Astrid never mentioned suicide again. She was far too bored to commit suicide. And they were both beyond something. He couldn't wait to see Astrid and try to sense whether or not it was true they were beyond everything.

He went to her, held her face in his hands, bent over and kissed her softly. "I've never stopped loving you," he said.

"Oh, great!" said Astrid. Joe felt the ache of tears come.

25

A man from the Soil Conservation Service came out in the morning and Joe walked him up the hill to show him where he wanted to put some concrete turn-outs and drop lines for his irrigating water. The man kept stuffing his lower lip with Copenhagen and staring out at the edge where the sagebrush breaks reached the brilliant green of the alfalfa. He had recently been through a divorce, he explained, and wasn't all there. Joe just couldn't stand to hear this. He was counting on this man to represent the real world right this very minute.

"We'll have to survey the ditches in again because we're burning up on the tops of all those knolls," Joe said. "I don't think they were ever in the right place."

"She took me to the cleaners," said the ASCS man, elevating the brim of his cap with a rigid forefinger. "She left me a purple pickup and one clean pair of jeans and that was all she wrote. Propped up in front of the game shows smoking weed all day and this baldheaded old judge says she gets the works."

"I hear you," said Joe absently, and tried to get back to his subject, which was an aging alfalfa field and a ditch that leaked because of all the shale. "The thing is, I've got some backhoe and concrete work that has to be done and it's going to be expensive."

But before he could enlarge on his subject, the government man said, "We'll pick up seventy percent on all irrigation projects whether you shit, go blind, or piss up a rope. But you're going to have to come to town and fill out some forms."

That was what Joe wanted. So he commenced a laying on of hands, murmuring effectively about the victim's life in America. The ASCS man told him the working man don't stand a chance. They walked down through the alfalfa, the white flowers just beginning to come, the shadows curving toward them over the plateau. A hawk flew levelly across the space toward a single tree; just before he got there, his line of flight took a deep sag and he swooped up to his perch.

Joe's cattle were such a sorry, mixed bunch, under such a variety of brands, that it was imperative to get them in and rebrand every one of them. The state brand inspector practically ordered him to. "You better have you a branding bee," he said to Joe when they looked over the receipts.

Joe branded a hundred and thirteen yearlings on Sunday. Astrid left early to tour Yellowstone. She had heard about branding and was determined, she said, to go through life without ever seeing it. Two strong neighbor boys, Ellen's nephews, came down to wrestle. Joe roped the whole time off his gelding, enjoying the good job of breaking Bill Smithwick had done. Old man Overstreet, his plaid overcoat safety-pinned across his chest, showed there were no hard feelings by helping Joe at head and heels as they worked the yearlings in the pole corral. But Joe remembered the old man had been told about Clara. Joe was a little uncomfortable.

Joe thought, I've been away too long. I feel sorry for these animals. A tall sixteen-year-old in a red shirt, which had rotted out in the center of his shoulders, followed the dragging cattle behind Joe's horse and grabbed a front leg so they would drag more smoothly. The other boy put a knee on the head and crimped a foreleg around. The sixteen-year-old sat on the ground holding one leg and subdued the other with his feet. Still, they got kicked. Old man Overstreet applied the irons, J-S, Joe's father's brand. When the smoking metal seared into the flesh of the steers, they stretched their necks out and opened their mouths; their gray tongues fell forth and they bawled. Joe could hardly bear it, though he let no expression cross his face. The sixteen-year-old freed Joe's lariat, and the boy's mother, a silent, rawboned woman of fifty, applied the iron and gave shots to the ones with hoof rot or bad eyes. It went very smoothly in an increasing cloud of smoke. When they had all the cattle penned in one place, old man Overstreet, looking like an undertaker in his long tattered coat, started to go through the cattle with his cutting horse.

Joe thanked his helpers and went back to the ranch to do the paperwork on the soil conservation cost-sharing application. There were black thunderheads up the valley and occasional sparks of lightning; the day could quickly get shortened. He cracked a beer and went out on the porch to watch the weather. This may be the principal use of a cattle ranch in these days, he thought: watching the weather. He daydreamed. Holding his cold can of beer, he remembered an old radio ad he had heard years ago in some city, an ad that was recited in a stylish, hip shout: *"Jet Malt Liquor! Acts much quicker! It leaves you flying at thirty thousand feet!"* Can't ask more of a beer than that. And now came the butterflies, drifting across from the orchard, fritillaries, sulphurs. Little messages from above. A mixed blessing, an easy life. It seemed unbearable that Astrid didn't enjoy this. A car surged past far across the fields on the highway, a big American flag streaming from its antenna.

26

There had been days down south, amazingly long and durable, the days of Joe and Astrid letting down their guards, that turned upon ordinariness. The wonderful times in the produce department of the supermarket, shopping for dinner; the same cheerful black woman sprayed mist on the bins of vegetables and it was like being on a pleasant, intensive truck farm. Or they sailed out to the swampy, uninhabited islands drifting past the bird-crowned mangroves, whose small white blossoms were aswarm with honey bees. They watched the tourists photograph the pelican. They watched the international white sea clouds arrive from Central America on southerly winds.

Sometimes they had helped each other home from bars where a stunned, reflexive criminality disclosed itself in the hungry night life. To have no plan, in the serene near-darkness, amid papery flowers that emerged at sundown, seemed all that they could desire. He had wanted Astrid to understand him. It frightened him to think he might not hate her. This pain seemed quite physical. He had begun picturing Astrid day and night. He had begun to be terrified for her well-being. It was horrible. He resumed cigarettes.

But the time came when it all seemed unhealthy. They withdrew to Green Turtle Cay. There they met a land surveyor from Ohio in a borrowed boat, who was thrown up on the beach by a gale. They sent the homemade local postcards to everyone they knew. They walked the beach at all hours and on Sunday stood in front of the local churches to hear the singing. From the telegraph hill, they could watch yachts move along the coast of Great Abaco, the passenger ferry's regular plying and the periodic advent of the tomato boat. On Wednesday, it was possible to observe the fabulously grotesque scuba lessons behind the one popular resort hotel. Coconut or fruit trees which had proven reliable had steps nailed to their trunks. Each day, swimming became more important. Joe wanted to stay in the cottage and have sex, while Astrid wished to paddle out a few yards for purposes of gaining contact with the drop-off. Finally, it threatened to spoil their vacation and they went back.

Joe made it a habit to ride through the yearlings every day. They were pretty well scattered out and it always took an entire morning. But he enjoyed saddling his horse in the dark and then to be rolling along as the day broke to count and check the cattle. Behind this was the knowledge that he really couldn't afford any death loss. The country had had several dry years; cattle numbers were down across the state, and in the Midwest it was rumored that stored feed was at an all-time high. Unless somebody fooled around with it and the futures boys manipulated things out of all reason, Joe thought his cattle would be right valuable by fall.

The great pleasure came from the grass, traveling through

HAILEY PUBLIC LIBRARY

it horseback: the movement of the wind on its surface, the blaze of sunrise across its ocean curves. As the full warmth of day came on, the land took on a humming vitality of cows and grass and hawks, and antelope receded dimly like something caught in your eye. Joe always rode straight into at least one covey of partridges which roared up around his horse. After the first burst, the little brick and gray chickens cast down onto a hillside and resumed feeding. Joe's horse watched hard, then went on traveling. Instead of being someplace where he waited for the breeze through a window, Joe had gone to where the breeze came from.

One day, walking into a dell in search of the head of a small spring, he sensed something in the chest-high grass and serviceberry patches. He stopped to listen. He looked straight up into the brightness of the afternoon sun as something stirred. Suddenly, two cinnamon cubs sprang upright into the glitter, weaving to scent him. As Joe began to back out the way he'd come in, the mother bear rose on her haunches, swinging her muzzle in an arc. The sun behind her made the edge of her coat ignite in a silvery veil. The cubs hastened to their mother's side and the three of them went up to the top of the spring and disappeared into the berry bushes. Joe was out of breath. He couldn't believe his luck in receiving such a gift.

The yearlings began to gain visibly. Joe cut back the chronic pinkeye and hoof-rot cattle until he had them cleaned up and returned to the herd. There was everything in this motley set of cheap cattle: blacks, black baldies, Herefords, Charolais, some Simmental crosses. It didn't matter. He and Lureen had kept their costs down and if the deer flies and nose flies didn't run the yearlings through the wire later on, they ought to do all right.

Most of the cattle were concentrated in the north-facing coulees where the snow had lingered late in the spring. Another mile toward the Yellowstone was the end of the property and the beginning of wild short-grass country, intersected by seasonal watercourses and cottonwood breaks. Here, three different times, Joe found his gate open, thrown defiantly out on the ground. He had a feeling Billy Kelton had passed this way. Luckily, the cattle never found the gap.

Astrid got sick to her stomach and then the sickness just went on and on. They both got nervous about it and finally Joe suggested she go in and see a doctor at the hospital. She hadn't been particularly healthy since she arrived. Nobody was on duty, so, in the end, she stayed at the hospital overnight.

Joe slept poorly, imagining the worst. He picked her up first thing in the morning. She fluttered her fingers in the doorways of other patients she had become acquainted with. In one room, an old man danced around wildly with a smile on his face. "He's on a natural high," said Astrid as they passed the room. Another patient, a woman over eighty, had been parked in a wheelchair and left near the pay phone. She stared at a fixed place in front of her and her eyes never moved when people passed before her. There was no way to tell that she was still alive. "She's so unjudgmental," Astrid said as she made her way fixedly toward the sunlight. Joe held a hand at her elbow and walked her down the sidewalk along the little dotted plantings of potentilla in the cool yellow sun. "I just can't tell you," she said. Joe could feel the thrill of release in her tremulous sighs. "Wouldn't it be something to go straight to the ocean? It was the last stop for some of those people. I felt it. I felt the time we're wasting."

Joe had to navigate the truck intently. The sun shining through the windshield heated up the cab, and the windvane hissed over the country-Western station.

"Have you been in touch with anybody?" Joe asked. There were a lot of phone calls on the bill when he checked Astrid out of the hospital.

"I called a few people last night. Then I quit. They were going to charge out here for a laying on of hands."

"Anything new?"

"Patti and G.J. got busted."

"No surprise there," Joe said.

"Mark Perkins bought a sportfisherman at the federal drug-boat auction. Supposed to have been a good buy."

"So what did the doctor say?"

"He said I've got colitis. He said it's from stress. They have some cortisone thing they can do but I said forget it, I'll try to deal with the causes. Big talk. Joe, I don't have any business being here."

Joe stared straight at the spot above the road where it all turned blue. "You're going to see the point of this soon," he said.

"That's why I came up here."

"Are you okay?"

"I don't know."

At the ends of the roads to the small ranches, people stood by their mailboxes looking through the mail. When Joe and Astrid were nearly home, they came upon a band of sheep swarming on the road. An old man with a long white beard followed the sheep on an ancient horse; his dogs swept back and forth keeping the sheep under control. A younger man walking out at the edge of the herd saw Joe and ran over. Swinging his arm for Joe to follow, he went up through the sea of sheep, causing a channel as wide as the road to part through the wool surface. Joe was able to drive through this as the sheep closed behind him, and in a minute he was beyond the band and up to road-speed again. Astrid watched with a smile. You could never tell what Astrid would like.

They drove into the ranch yard. The dog retreated to a juniper and stared indifferently. Joe jumped out of the truck and, crossing in front of the hood, turned to face Astrid through the windshield. Joe felt she'd been away for years. He spread his arms in welcome. A terrific smile consumed his features. Astrid lit a cigarette and pushed the windvane open while she watched Joe.

"Baby, we're home!" he cried. He thought the pain of his love for Astrid would be more than he could stand.

Joe arranged to meet Smitty at the dining room of the Bellwood Hotel and got a table off to themselves. From the lobby, Joe had watched Smitty drive up in a Cadillac. The car was so astonishing and had such power to undermine any subsequent conversation that Joe hurried into the dining room to prevent Smitty's knowing he had seen it. In this small town, a new Cadillac was an item of almost exaggerated splendor and dimension and had the effect of a cruise liner on remote native populations. Joe feared that Smitty had been unable to live up to this new vehicle, and under Joe's gaze would slink from its interior in defeat.

But Joe was wrong. Smitty appeared in the doorway to the dining room, chucked the waitress under the chin, and waved the leather tab of his car keys at Joe. "Joe boy," he called, waltzing toward him. "Am I late?"

"Oh no, Smitty, you're not late. You're on time."

Smitty hung his coat over the back of his chair and sat down with a bounce. "Who do you have to fuck to get a drink around here?" he inquired, letting his eyes drift to the royal elk over the entryway to the kitchen. A waitress emerged and Smitty arrested her with a grin. "My nephew and I would like a sarsaparilla." The waitress took their orders and when she was gone, Smitty said, "There's a side to my drinking, I admit it's small, that I really enjoy. Isn't that surprising? After all these years? A side to this disease that I'd hate to see changed." This moment all but took the wind from Joe's sails. When the drinks arrived, Smitty held his glass of sour mash to the light and said, "You have no idea what this looks like to me. I do not see an instrument of torture. I see something more golden than any casket in the Theban tombs. Knowing that it will kill me in the end, I see the purest, most priceless ambergris of the Arctic cetaceans, the jewel in the crown, the pot of gold at the end of the rainbow. Does it bother me that I will die in abject misery, shaking myself to death in delirium? I have to be honest: *not right now it doesn't*. It's a strong man's weakness."

"I've been to the insurance people," Joe said. "We're going to have to settle with them."

"Why?"

"Because you'll go to jail if they press charges. The insurance company still won't pay. Lureen would be miserable without you. And it is not customary to serve cocktails in jail."

"What do you think, Joe?"

"I think you're guilty. Lureen's your ace in the hole."

"Yours too, Joe."

"I don't think so."

"Don't you? Whose ranch is that?"

"Mine."

"Really?" said Smitty. "Say, I knew your father very well and I don't really buy all this. He didn't like you much, my friend." Smitty's incredibly wrinkled, almost Eurasian face split into

175

laughter. Joe thought of the word "dynamite" as it was used a few years ago. He thought that Smitty had a dynamite laugh, except that it made Joe want to dynamite Smitty. He was weary of trying to understand Smitty. He had just seen a child abusers' support group on television. It seemed society didn't understand their need to beat children. It was getting harder and harder to be understanding. It had always been a problem but now the problem was almost out of sight. Smitty was capable of love, he'd heard; but Smitty's great drive was to get out of the rain. It was hard to understand Smitty completely and not hope his dynamite laugh blew up in his face.

"Let me ask you something, Smitty. Did you borrow the money for the shrimp against the ranch?"

"Yes I did," he said smartly.

"And is there any left?"

"Not much!"

"I see." It was going to have to be a great year for cattle. A century record.

"And I presume you'd just as soon concede that the insurance company has a point."

"That'd be fine."

Of course, thought Joe, let's be honest. Smitty had challenged Joe's claims to the ranch. He didn't know whether or not he cared; but at least he knew he should care. Moreover, he'd be damned if it was Smitty's to decide. On the other hand, as the booze hit Smitty and began its honeyed rush through his bloodstream, he slumped into vacancy and into the great mellow distances past judgment. Joe had been around alcoholism all his life but didn't really understand it. Liquor was just a pleasant thing to him, possessed of no urgency; he would never have resisted Prohibition. It just didn't matter to him as it did to his parents or to Smitty, who was bound for glory.

When Smitty resumed speech it was in a mellifluous tone. "I knew with the loss of the lease," he said, "something had to be done. And you were the one to do it. I also knew that it was not necessary, technically, for you and Lureen to consult with me —"

"You were much occupied with the seafood business —"

"— but I am family, and I would like to be kept abreast of things."

"You will be."

"Our vital interests are now tied together, at least emotionally, and when you buy cattle with the ranch as collateral, I should be told."

"Hereafter, you will be."

"And when you sell those cattle —"

"Yes."

"Just tell me."

"We will."

"I would like to accompany those cattle to the auction yard."

"You may conduct the sale yourself," Joe said feelingly at the sight of Smitty's twitching face, the watery blue eyes seeming to plead for a stay of execution. "Once we bring those cattle down off that grass, I will have done all I could."

Smitty rested the nail of his right forefinger on the rim of his glass. "Along about when?" It was only then that Joe suspected Smitty's intentions exactly.

"October fifteenth," said Joe. There was now no one else in the restaurant; the two sat in its streaming vacancy as though they were in a great train station on the edge of empty country. "Lureen and me," said Smitty, musing. "I don't know. Our mother was a saint, an uncrowned saint. And our father. Um. A short-fused man with a little white mark in his eye. Kind of blind in that one, he was. He used to whup your dad till he was black and blue. Supposed to have made a man out of him. What's that mean, anyway?" Joe didn't know. He wasn't thinking of the question, really. He had just had a presentiment of disaster.

28

As Joe drove home, his mind wandered back a year or so and, as though for the first time, he could see Astrid, her very real beauty, the peculiar elegance of her every gesture, the air of mystery lent her by a gene pool across the Gulf Stream, the saddest river of them all, where some of the world's most interesting races fell into the sugar kettle together. As he dodged the small cattle trucks on the way, he asked himself if he was remembering this right, about Astrid's presence, if that was what it was, her aura, her allure, and if it was still there at all, through the intervening history.

When he drove into the yard, Astrid was knocking apples out of a tree with a stick. She stopped and leaned on the stick to watch him come in. He looked at her. It was still there.

Astrid felt good enough, it seemed. Joe had to take the position that the stress and colitis were gone and now she was better. She immediately made an attempt to fully inhabit the house, to rearrange it, and make it her own. This produced a pleasant feeling in Joe and he was happy to move furniture as instructed and even to dust the tops of tables and bureaus, and the surfaces of the venetian blinds. Astrid had been raised in a conventional Cuban-exile household in Florida, had duly celebrated her *quince* in the tarted-up strumpet costumes that suggested the elders were putting their daughters on the open market. Her life until then had made a regular little wife-prospect of her, but an American high school and four years at Gainesville had flung her into the future. Astrid's latinity became a romantic feature as she went from hippie spitfire to a goddess of the Florida night. Anglo girls in her company always seemed to feel both hygienic and anesthetized. Astrid liked that. She called them "white girls." Now she was up on the sagebrush prairie getting over a broken heart. In a short while, they would both be on social security, trying to eat corn on the cob with ill-fitting dentures. If there is reincarnation, Joe thought, I want to come back as a no-see-um.

They sat down to dinner right after sunset. Coyotes came down close to the yard and howled back and forth. Astrid put the serving dishes on the table: black beans, yellow rice, chicken. Joe lit the candles. "That would be your coyotes?" Astrid asked, at the latest uproar outside the windows. Joe nodded. "You know," she said, "I'm sort of beginning to appreciate this place." She looked off. "Sort of."

"Good," said Joe, gazing in rapture at the tropical food.

"But this country, it's the big romance in your life, isn't it?"

"For what it's worth."

"The mountains?"

"I don't particularly like the mountains," said Joe.

"You like all that other stuff. The stuff that doesn't look like anything. The prairie."

"Yep."

"Because why? Because it makes you feel big or because it makes you feel little?"

"Jesus, Astrid, how should I know? You don't necessarily like things on the basis of the size they make you feel."

"Very well," said Astrid. Joe looked at her blinding and mischievous smile. He could feel his pulse racing.

"What a meal," said Joe. "Like we never left."

"Really, you left," said Astrid.

"I guess."

"I followed."

"It's sweet, isn't it."

"Because you stole my car."

"Yes . . ."

"And because you hated me," Astrid said.

"You followed because I hated you?"

"Hated me enough to steal from me."

"Oh, let's not make more of this than there really is. I needed to get home and my sense of style precluded catching the old outbound dog. Do you mind if we finish this nice meal before we pursue this?"

"You can't hate and eat at the same time?" Astrid asked.

"I can if I have to."

They were nearly finished eating. The rich dishes had left a lovely sheen on the plates.

"I wonder if there is some way we can have sex," Astrid said. Joe felt a sudden tension in his stomach.

"It's really up to you, I —"

"My God, Joe, you're hard already!"

"Not for long, my darling."

Astrid covered her face and let out a Cuban-coyote laugh of extreme merriness. When she was quiet, she allowed her eyes to gaze back. "It's still there."

"Astrid."

"The unsightly bulge of legend," said Astrid. "We'll have to be very gentle."

"Look!" Joe shouted as he stood up and pointed to his trousers. "This time it *is* gone!"

Joe began to clear the table. He didn't like all these jokes. He rinsed off the dishes and thought how he disliked sharing chores. And he'd long since decided it was easier to eat out than show gratitude for home cooking. He'd rather do it all himself, or have somebody else do it all while he did something entirely different but complementary and useful. He wouldn't mind looking after Astrid but he preferred doing it all. In general, he was appalled by the various duos: Butch Cassidy and the Sundance Kid, Bonnie and Clyde, the Reagans. He looked around him and all he saw were these duos. It was like needing the prescription changed in your reading glasses; the world was made incoherent by duos or by people trying to cook side by side.

By the time Joe followed Astrid into the bedroom, she had undressed and was stretched out on top of the blankets. There was a small lamp in one corner with desert scenes depicted on its shade that gave only a small amount of light. He undressed and lay beside her. He put his hand on her and she closed her eyes. The light seemed to waver as he felt the wetness begin around his fingers. She tipped her legs open. He heard the coyotes start in again. He slipped down between her thighs and put his tongue inside her. When he moved up, she said, "You may now enter," and he did. She pressed upward and shuddered; he sometimes felt that the Latin woman in Astrid was revealed in the indignation of her orgasm. Then he came and it was suddenly almost impossible to keep his weight off her, the feeling of an external force using then discarding him.

"I'm hungry again," Joe said after a bit.

"Real hungry?"

"For a snack."

"Make some toast. There's some preserves in the fridge."

"I love the word 'fridge.' "

"Make me a piece too."

"Like a fridge over troubled waters," sang Joe.

"How can you be so happy with someone you hate?" Astrid said.

Joe looked at the toaster with its astounding automotive shape, its haunted black slots now showing the faintest smoke of the toast inside. He examined the glints on the toaster and found little curved details of his house. When it popped up, he buttered the toast and spread strawberry preserves. He headed back to the bedroom. Every other woman he ever knew now bored him.

"You ought to put on some pants," Astrid said, "if you're going to serve food."

"You can't please everyone."

"It's waving around."

"It's not 'waving around.' "

He went to the window to look at the full moon. Everything was so clear, it was as if he was right out there with the moon. The stars showed in great sheets like the spray from a breaking wave. Beneath them were the curves of the prairie. Joe ate his toast and jam in the window and watched. He didn't think it made man seem small to see the vastness of the natural world. I'm just going to stand here, he thought, drained of sperm, my brain in the constellations.

"I don't know if I ever told you this, Astrid," Joe said, turning back toward the bed. "But I used to be a pretty darn good caddy. I was captain of all the caddies when I was sixteen years old. Carried double with those big old leather bags. Nine out of ten of those golfers let me pick their clubs. I never played myself. I was saving up for college. My father could afford to send me to college but his drinking had made him so erratic, I wasn't sure he would keep it together until I got there. Sure enough, he went tits-up on a land development deal and I was lucky to have my caddy savings. One time, I tried to help him. He was such a good fellow when he was sober that I was sure he had no idea of how he acted when he was drinking. So I bought a tape recorder and spent the evening with him. He went crazier than usual. The next day, while he was still hung over, I brought the tape into his bedroom, set it up on the dresser and turned it on real loud. Well, it should have worked. As a theory it was very much in the ballpark. But the actual sound of his own ranting and raving was much more than he could deal with. He bellowed. He smashed the machine. He kicked me out of the house. Not long afterward, he drank himself to death. Possibly, that is where he was headed. Sometimes I think I murdered my father with his own voice."

"What got us started on this?"

"I look out at the stars and wonder if my folks are out there."

"I see."

"All their troubles gone."

Joe got in under the covers next to Astrid. He turned on the bedside radio. A man was describing his visit to the great mall of Edmonton, Alberta. Joe lay with Astrid considering this mall in their warmth. The man couldn't fully express the size of the great mall to the listening audience. He had picked out a shirt he liked in a men's store in the mall. He went out to be sure that there wasn't another shirt in another store, in another part of the mall, he might prefer. He concluded that it was the original shirt, a blue Western-cut shirt with snap buttons, that he wanted more than the other shirts, many nice ones — there's no disputing taste! — he had seen. But the great mall of Edmonton, Alberta, was so vast, so labyrinthine, that he could never find the store again that sold the shirt he preferred. Question for the listening audience: can a mall be, somehow, too wonderful, too big? Specifically, does the great mall of Edmonton, Alberta, so surpass our hopes that we are no longer satisfied by it? Stay tuned.

Joe and Astrid were asleep.

Joe wondered what brought these tranquil eras on. There hadn't been many of them. He'd once had one that lasted a whole winter in the Hotel Dixie in New York. He'd been painting; he'd had a nice plant, girlfriends, no vices, clients, tickets to fights and shows, surprising acquaintances. Then homesickness struck. The plant which had seemed so companionable turned into a vile hothouse puke overnight. Suddenly, he was stoned day after day. The girlfriends were reptiles. When they made love, all he noticed was their frightening shadows on the ceiling from the streetlight outside the window. The fights, shows, and companions were maddeningly predictable. Some of his work seemed senseless no matter how much it was accepted. He even tried to capture the white hills. The era of tranquillity dissolved and his wanderings began anew. He hoped the present state wouldn't disappear the same way.

The cattle looked so fine scattered out on the grass and the springs were flowing at such a good rate, that Joe, out of pride, gave Lureen a tour, driving through the pastures in the truck and noting the atmosphere of renewed prosperity. She peered peakedly out at the ranch, her face low in the window of the truck.

"How much are they going to make us?" Lureen wanted to know.

"We'll find out when we get to the sale yard."

"But they always used to tell me ahead of time. I could just call that nice Mr. Overstreet and he'd tell me."

"That was a lease, Lureen. We didn't own the cattle. And Mr. Overstreet isn't what you think he is."

"I just don't know," she said. They drove on past the sheep-herders' monument to the low breaks that looked off toward the Crazies. Some cattle were brushed up in the midday and a coyote angled away from them, stopping every few yards to look back. The truck labored in first gear and Lureen held on to her seat with both hands. There were two short-eared owls coursing over the sagebrush for mice and one distant hill had the outline of a band of antelope serrated on its crest. What am I saying by this, Joe wondered. That it is mine? The owls curved on around toward the truck, their pale, flat faces cupped toward the ground. Their wings beat steadily and they moved at the speed of a man walking.

"I could have done without this," said Lureen. "Your father pushed me around when he put it in my hands. In a way, I never wanted it. I worked all my life. I didn't want to be pushed around. Then Smitty had so much bad luck. The war hurt him. The war all but killed Smitty. And I had to help him, more than I could have without this."

"Does Smitty realize the war is over?"

"I really couldn't say."

"What does he want, Aunt Lureen?"

187

She thought. She looked out through the windshield at the country Joe liked so much. The country seemed to wither as she looked at it, the springs stopping and the steady wind carrying the life out of everything.

"I think Smitty would prefer to be somewhere where he could be warmer. He thinks a lot about falling on the ice."

That would be about right, Joe thought.

"Do you see how fat those yearlings look?" he asked.

She looked blank. Fat cattle were the local religion. They were the glow, the index of this place. If one didn't care about fat cattle, this was not the place to be. It should not have been necessary to find words for it. It was annoying to find yourself trying to communicate the glow of a particular country to someone with a blank look on her face.

Lureen kept looking out the window and trying to be interested. She put a finger to her cheek when they passed a few yearlings standing alongside the road and said, "Mmm!" like someone tasting a candy bar in a commercial.

When he got back from dropping Lureen off, a bundle of steel posts and barbed wire in the back, Astrid was down alongside the creek looking into a pool. "I can see the fish!" she called. Joe parked and walked down beside her. They sat on a sun-warmed boulder. "This is pretty nice," Astrid said. "The birds shoot back and forth across the creek. It's like there are two bird countries and they visit each other. There's also one that walks down the bank and disappears under water. Am I hallucinating?"

"It's a dipper."

"Well, no one lives quite like the dipper. Give me a hug."

Joe squeezed her. She slid down from the rock and stood embracing him, her face turned sideways on his chest. She held him that way for a moment then pulled her dress over her hips and pressed against him. "Here?" he said.

"I think so," she said. As they made love, he felt with his fingertips where the warm granite was pressed against her flesh. Later they dressed and followed the stream up for a couple of miles. There were teal in the backwaters and they saw a young mink darting in and out of the exposed cottonwood roots along the bank. Joe told Astrid what it was and she wanted to know how many it took to make a coat.

"Have you noticed something?" Astrid asked.

"What?"

"I'm still here."

"I did notice that!"

The Butterfields down the road past the Overstreets had a siege of dust emphysema go through their calves, and everyone chipped in to doctor. Joe helped move cattle down the alley to the chute, and afterward he spent a few hours hunting arrowheads. Joe remembered the time he fell down a hole, knocked himself in the head, and dreamed that he was an Indian attacking his own home. When he looked for arrowheads, it was with a ticklish feeling that he was searching for part of his own earlier life. He stopped at eighty-year-old Alvie Butterfield's little house to ask permission to hunt in his recently spaded-up garden. Alvie's garden happened to be a camp where Indians had dropped projectiles from Folsom points all the way up to Winchester cartridges from the Victorian age, continuous occupancy for thousands of years. It was just a garden to Alvie, who was getting ready to join those warriors in what the Indians called "the other side camp." Standing reedily in a baseball cap, Alvie Butterfield waited for the end.

"I left 'em all for you," said Alvie.

"Attaboy."

"You got a TV?"

"Yes, I do," said Joe.

"What's it supposed to do?"

"Rain by Wednesday."

"Good."

"You need anything, Alvie?"

"Not really, no."

Joe went out to Alvie's garden spot. There were the weed-less hand-spaded rows. There were the curves of earth where the shovel had left them in the ancient camp. Many a rare plan was laid here. The new sun was sucking the moisture from around the eloquent flints. Joe began to walk the rows like a stoop worker at a lettuce farm. Each row unraveled beneath his eyes slowly, the approximate straight lines of Alvie's shovel converted to amazing canyons, the clay banding the loam wherever it fell, numerous rocks. Joe had never much cared for rocks. They were merely the increasingly magnifying context of what man had not made. Too many rocks were annoying. Joe had been dutiful about going around with a field geology guide but it had not taken. The rocks and soil were just the old land as received. His mind filled with their tumbled shapes as he made his slow way up and down the rows with intermittent hopes over stones that had accidentally split. A circle of warmth expanded between his shoulders. Alvie's radio played from afar. A band of birds went through the air like a cluster of buckshot. He found places where Alvie in his weariness had rested on the shovel, the blade penetrating without lifting. For a long time, Joe felt himself to be in a place in the earth where no one had ever lived; a few flakes of brighter, prizeable stone like a thin pulse began to turn up and suddenly life surged: *an arrowhead.* Joe picked it up and blew the grains of dirt off of it, a bird point, notched, shaped, a little weight in the palm, something he wanted to close his hand around to feel the life in it. He was as possessive as the man who had lost it. It was just a moment, as if they could feel each other through the stone.

Then some of Joe's cattle got through the fence and traveled a couple of miles to the bottom of a big coulee where they loafed in the ruins of an old homestead. Joe tried to bring them back but ended up having to get Freddy Mathias and one of the Lovells' high school kids to help him. It made a nice day horseback, whooping and riding through the rough country, the yearlings running erratically in front of them with their tails straight up in alarm. The southern migration of birds of prey had begun and there was an archival assortment of hawks on the crooked cedar posts. A golden eagle towered over the ranch, slipping from lift to lift till he went through the roof of heaven. The high school boy took a header at a gallop, a burst of dust; the tough kid scrambled to run down his horse and remount. Freddy went past Joe at a conservative trot and, when he saw the youngster snatch up his horse, said, "Oh, to be young again!"

When they pushed the yearlings back through the gap in the fence, the cattle quit running so hard and seemed to admit they knew they were back where they were supposed to be. Joe looked around. They were only a few thousand feet above the old homestead but it seemed like the roof of the world. He could look off not so far and see the granite verticals, the permanent snow. The world here seemed like a real planet and not just the physical excrescence of civilization.

When the youngster rode up, Joe said, "You break anything?"

"Naw."

"What happened?"

"Sonofabitch lit in a anthill."

Joe thanked them and everybody split up on their shortcuts home, the three horses quickly disappearing from each other in the back country. Joe returned to patch the hole in the fence and started back. The scent of ditch-burning was in the air, like burning leaves in small towns in the fall. The country just seemed to drop away from the horse in a pleasant way. Joe picked up the old wagon road for the last mile and a half, and jogged back down to the buildings, arriving at the moment the nighthawks swarmed into dusk.

At Lureen's request, he stopped in to see her in the blue house that lost more of its power to haunt him the longer he was home. The ghosts of cellar and attic were eclipsed by the need for repairs, and the oversize kitchen stove only empha-sized Lureen's paltry cooking talents. As he drove up to the house, he saw Smitty's face briefly in the window. He knocked and Lureen came to the door.

When Joe asked after Smitty, Lureen said he was in Wolf Point visiting Sioux and Assiniboine members of the Veterans of Foreign Wars. They sat down to tea. Lureen wasn't saying much but she looked scared. On a table next to the dining room door was a substantial pile of new clothes, men's and women's, curious because they were strictly for tropical wear. "Sale items," said Lureen, seeing Joe look. He had never seen such colors in this house. It was as if the coconuts of the space program had come back to haunt him.

"I have something for you," Lureen said and left the room. While she was gone, Joe tried to guess what gruesome family memento would soon be his. He drank the tea he had never liked. He looked at walls which had first defined interior space to him, then had filled him with a lifetime's claustrophobia. He looked out the high windows beside the kitchen door to the blue sky and felt all over again that freedom could very well be at hand.

Lureen came back in and placed a file folder on the table. He suddenly knew what it was. It was the deed. In her own way, Lureen was making every cent count. She knew Smitty was going to take the check for the yearlings. Joe was filled with nervous excitement. Smitty and Lureen were going to Hawaii with the check. Between that and the money lost on Smitty's seafood venture, the place would be bankrupt. And he held the deed in his hands. "The transfer is in there, and it's been notarized."

"How can I thank you?" he asked. Slipping eye contact, a tremor crossing Lureen's face, and the dissolute nephew receiving a family holding, in vacuity, with hands he hoped expressed as much sincerity as the praying hands on Christmas cards. All in their way were the last detectable tremors of the life of a family. Joe looked down at the empty document, thinking it might contain a single ounce of meaning or reality or possibility by way of naming or holding a place on earth, and he was suddenly and absurdly elated. He looked at Lureen, divested of the ranch, and he saw in her eyes a dream lighter and more ethereal than Hawaii itself. It was as if in this room where the hopes of generations had just collapsed, the roar of warm surf could be heard. He couldn't keep the mad grin off his face, the goofy and vaguely celebratory grin that Lureen observed in astonishment.

30

It was just starting to get cold. The local weather forecasts were revised twice a day as the weathermen of three different channels strove against one another in explaining the Rorschach shapes of storms in the Gulf of Alaska. Joe concentrated on the fates of these storms as they threw themselves on the mountains of Washington and Idaho, and expired. One of these days soon, they were going to slide down through Alberta, catch the east side of the Rockies, and turn Joe's world upside down.

He took this time to cut firewood and spent days on end in the cottonwood groves taking out the standing dead and transporting the wood to a pile next to the house. The growth of this pile fascinated him. He sensed it was in his power to make a pile bigger than the house. He moved along the creek and cut up the trees the beavers had felled. While he worked, he could see trout on the redds, swirling after one another and fanning nests into the gravel. The eagles had started coming in from the north and were standing high in the bare trees along the stream. Their rapine, white-tailed, dark and monkish shapes showed from a quarter of a mile away.

He sat down in the autumn forest, an old woodchopper with his hot orange chain saw. I am posing for eternity, he thought. He was desperate. He was desperate because the constant companionship of unanswered questions was affecting his nerves and suggesting that it was the absolute final and daily condition of living. He was no longer interested in remaining in the space program.

The irrigation water stopped running and the springs were down to a bare minimum. He moved the yearlings every few days, an activity that took him to remote pastures on horseback. He enjoyed his horse's sure-footedness. He could travel on breathtaking sidehills you could barely negotiate on your own feet in a kind of skywalking perfection as the cattle flew forward in coveys. In this motion and vastness, he could actually think about life, beginning and end, with equanimity, with cheer. Joe thought he was vaguely bigger than everything he saw and therefore it would be tragic and for all nations to weep over, if anything happened to him. But here in the hills, he would feed the prettiest birds. As promised by all religions, he would go up into the sky where his folks were.

Joe felt the return of love and remorse, like a bubble of gas rising through crankcase residue. The slowness of the bubble's traverse seemed to express the utter gallonage of his desire as well as the regret that made it something of a rich dish and gave this emotion its peculiar morning-after quality.

"I think we're missing something," he said.

After a moment, Astrid said, "I know what you mean."

She bit her thumbnail in thought and looked off. Joe examined some carpet. The white hills, the departing dream, the impending embarkation for Hawaii only illumined the plight. He had heard nothing from Ellen and felt she didn't want him to see Clara. When you're young and think you'll live forever, it's easy to think life means nothing.

Astrid stood up and stretched, then stopped all motion to smile at Joe. She went to the door and opened it, letting in the clear, balsamic breath of foothills, of sage and juniper and prairie grass. She stood on tiptoes to stretch and inhale.

"Joe," she said deliberately, "this isn't for me."

Joe didn't hear her. He turned on the radio. First he got a semi-intellectual cornball on FM and then a wonderful song from 1944 — what could that have been like! — about a cowboy going East to see the girl he loves best. "Graceful faceful" went the chorus, "such lovely hair! Oh, little choo-choo, please get me there!" It was sung in the kind of voice you'd use to call a dog in the dark when you really didn't expect the dog to come. It disturbed Joe because it suggested that the Americans of the recent past were insane foreigners. Then an ad for a local car dealer filled with apparently living objects: "Cold weather is coming and your car doesn't want to face it. You need a new one but your wallet says 'No'!" Joe thought, Is anyone following this? Astrid was still in the doorway. What was it she'd said?

There was no great problem in getting the criminal charges against Smitty dropped. Once Joe relieved the insurance company's fears of damage claims, once those assurances were documented and in place, the ripple of society's desire for retribution expired on the bench of the small, local court-house. Nevertheless, a few motions had to be gone through. Joe drove Smitty to the hearing as though he were his child and had been involved in a minor scrape. There was only the judge, dressed in the plaid wool shirt in which he had been raking leaves, and his secretary. Smitty appeared in his uniform and stood at attention throughout the questioning. So great was the judge's pity for this foolish person that he concluded his inquiry with the question "Can I count on you to avoid this kind of thing in the future, Lieutenant?"

"Yes, sir! You can, sir!"

The judge gazed down at Smitty with a melancholy smile. "Smitty, Smitty, Smitty," he said. "You're kind of dumb like a fox, aren't you?"

"Possibly so, yes, sir."

"Thank your lucky stars, Smitty, that you live in a small town where we know you for what you are. Adjourned."

Driving along to his meeting at the bank, Joe remembered his happiest period as a painter. One summer, he had gone on the road to do portraits of Little Leaguers. He set up a table at ballgames all over Montana and saw the rise and ripening of the great mountain summer from a hundred small-town diamonds. Instead of pumping gas or choking on dust behind a bale wagon, Joe turned out bright portraits of children in baseball uniforms. It was an opulent spell that Joe remembered now with a kind of agony.

Darryl Burke, Joe's banker, leaned back and laced his fingers behind his head. He wore a great blousy pin-striped blue and white shirt. "How's life on the haunted ranch?"

"Great for me. I'm a ghost myself."

"Bankers don't believe in ghosts. Bankers believe in the enforceability of contracts."

Joe didn't think this was the time to depict his dream of letting it all go back to the Indians by way of atoning for a century of abuses; nor to unleash his misogyny on family matters.

Darryl, his chair tilted back on two legs, pitched forward on four. "Do you know why Lureen lost her lease with Overstreet?"

"Not really. I figured everybody had all the grass they wanted."

"They lost their lease because Overstreet heard you were coming back."

"I'm not following this. What's that have to do with it?"

"Well, old Smitty had a double deal going there with old man Overstreet. When he couldn't get that ranch off your dad, he tried to get it off Lureen. Smitty wanted to make a deal but all he could control was the lease. As long as you weren't around. A lease for Smitty and a lease for Lureen. His was bigger."

Joe thought for a long moment before saying, "That's awful. I mean, I know it's awful. But if you and I were to go dig into it, we'd find out that Lureen was just looking the other way, happy that Smitty was staying busy. Still, you don't like to hear a thing like that."

"Of course you don't. And we're talking property here, man. When are you going to ship the cattle?"

"Pretty soon. But I'm hesitant."

"Hesitant? Now is the hour! This is the best the market is ever going to be."

"I think they're going to run off with the money."

"Who?"

"Smitty and Lureen."

"No, Joe, you don't think that. You just think you think that. That's crook time."

"They already have Hawaiian costumes. I've seen them."

"Come on. You mean that's where you think they're headed?"

Joe had his hands close to his chest and he pantomimed the playing of a ukulele. "Surf's up," he said grimly. Darryl stood and pulled down part of the venetian blinds so he could look out toward the drive-up tellers.

"Smitty will never run out of ideas," he said. "He's a fart in a skillet. But this is way past him. I don't see him making such a big move."

"He is concerned about falling on the ice. He wants to be warm."

"But," said Darryl, "when you get right down to it, if that's what they want to do, they can do it. They can. It might be the end of the ranch. But they can do it. If that's what they want. We covered our bet when we loaned money for the cattle. If Lureen wants to exchange those yearlings, and the money she borrowed for Smitty's shrimp deal, for the ranch itself, she can do it. Don't look at me, look at your father. I just keep score."

Suddenly, it came to Joe. "It's not fair!" he said. He decided he wouldn't mention that the deed, together with all its liens and encumbrances and appurtenances thereto, was in his pocket, thick as a week's worth of junk mail. In some opaque recess within Joe, a worm was turning. Property!

"I better get going," he said. "Thanks for visiting with me about this."

"Glad to, Joe. It's pretty clear, anyway."

"Try to come out and see us before it snows."

"What happened to summer? It's really hard to believe it could snow already."

"Do you actually notice such things from in here?" Joe asked. Darryl stared.

"I get out once in a while," he said.

31

In the dream it was summer and when he awakened he remembered the lazy sound of a small airplane and the sight of a little girl too far away to see clearly, picking chokecherries on the side of a ravine. The prairie spread into the distance and its great emptiness was not cheerful. It woke him up with sharp and undefined sadness. He tipped his watch, lying on the table beside the bed, so he could see its dial against the vague light coming in the window. It wasn't quite five yet. He lay back and felt the warmth of Astrid beside him. He knew he had to see Clara. He couldn't wait. He had thought his situation with Ellen would sort itself out and an appropriate introduction would ensue. But it seemed now that might never happen. He couldn't wait any longer.

He would go to the end of the Keltons' road and watch Clara get on the school bus. He arose slowly and began to dress. His stealth awakened Astrid. "What is it, honey?"

"I've got to get receipts for those cattle. I'm meeting the brand inspector at the scale house."

"When will you be back?"

"Before lunch." He felt something sharp from the deceit.

Joe left the truck almost two miles away from the Keltons' road just as the sun began to come up. He hurried along the oiled county road straight toward the lime and orange glow that in a matter of minutes would be the new day. When the sun finally did emerge, Joe was safely concealed in the scrub trees opposite Ellen and Billy's mailbox. He had a feeling he couldn't uncover. Waiting for his little girl to catch the school bus, he was as close to whole as he had felt in memory. It was several blissful moments before the absurdity of his situation, his concealment, his uncertain expectations, dissolved his well-being. The chill of morning crept in. Finally, the yellow school bus rose upon the crown of the hill and went right on through without stopping, as though it never stopped here. Did Ellen invent Clara? Joe thought of that first.

He crossed the county road and started up the ranch driveway, walking as quietly as he could so that he could hear if anyone approached. As he went along, presumably getting closer, his nervousness increased and he began to picture alert dogs bounding at him, a family bursting from the front door to confront a stranger.

By the time the house was visible, a modest white frame house, neatly tended, a few yards from its barns and outbuildings, Joe could see in a small grove of wild apple trees the perfect place to hide. A rooster crowed. And when he got inside the trees, his concealment was so perfect that he arranged his sweater against a tree trunk as a pillow and prepared to spend however long it took to watch every single human being who lived in that house, who used its front door, who walked in its yard, who did its chores.

The rooster crowed again and in the near distance a bull bellowed rhythmically. Past the house was a small corral. A solitary paint horse rolled and made a dust cloud, then stood and shook. In the sky above the house, just now ignited by sunrise, were clouds which must have hung there in the windless air all night long. Joe felt himself drift into this serenity as though, not merely hidden, he was incorporeal and free as a spirit.

The door opened and a little girl ran out, pursued by Billy. He overtook her, turned her, and rebuttoned her cloth coat. He pulled her straw hat down close on her head and she tipped it back again. He pulled it down and she tipped it back. He swept her up. He held her at arm's length where she hung like a rag doll with a grin on her face. She acted almost like a baby with Billy though she was far too old for that. Above all, she clearly resembled her father, Billy Kelton. Joe scarcely had time to track his astonishment. It was enough that Billy's olive skin was there and the distinctive, inset brown eyes. But the minute Clara spoke, asking Billy to let out some chickens, Joe knew from her crooning voice that Clara was feebleminded. Billy planted her where she stood and went into a low shed. There was an immediate squawking from within and then four or five hens ran into the yard. Clara ran after them. Billy came out and deftly swept up a small speckled hen. Clara took it in her arms. Billy removed her hat, kissed the crown of her head, and replaced the hat. He went back into the shed while Clara stood bundling the hen and rubbing her cheek against it. The little chicken sank her head between the shoulders of her wings. Billy emerged with some eggs held against his stomach with his hand.

"Let's eat, kid. Put your friend down."

"I want take my hen!" Clara crooned.

"Mama won't let us, angel," said Billy, wincing sympathetically.

"My friend!" she pleaded.

"Okay, go on and take her in the house," said Billy gently. "What d'you think Mama's gonna say? I'll tell you what Mama's gonna say. Mama's gonna say take that chicken on out of here."

Clara shrugged and followed Billy toward the house, defiantly carrying her hen. Billy went in and Clara hesitated. When the coast was clear, she set the hen down and made a haughty entrance to the house. The speckled hen shot erratically back to the shed. Joe didn't move. He felt compassion sweep over him, not for Clara, whom he did not know, but for Billy in all his isolated, violent ignorance. It was this Joe had waited for: something that would cross his mind like a change of weather and leave a different atmosphere behind.

32

The sun couldn't quite penetrate the pale gray sky. It looked as if it might rain; if it did, it would be a cold rain, close to snow. Everything about the morning said the season was changing fast. When Joe awoke, he felt a lightness that approached giddiness, almost a gaiety. It seemed so beyond sense that he thought he must immediately put it to use.

He got on the telephone and began calling truckers to haul his yearlings to the sale yard. He got a mileage rate, a loaded rate, and a deadhead surcharge. He arranged a dawn departure. The only thing to slow this cattle drive down was going to be the speed limit.

He spent the next day on horseback. Overstreet's nephews came up from their ranch as they had done for the branding and helped him gather his pastures. A small herd formed, then grew as he traveled forward, downhill and toward the corrals. The horses loved this and tossed their heads, strained at their bits, ran quartering forward, and generally hurled themselves into the work of sweeping the land of beef. Every now and again, a herd-quitter gave the men the excuse of a wild ride to restore the yearling to the mass of its fellows. By nightfall, the dust-caked nephews with the thin crooked mouths of their grandfather had started down the road home on lathered horses, and the cattle were quiet in the corrals. Overstreet himself was there to count the yearlings, mouthing the numbers and dropping his arm decisively every ten head. Looking at the backs and heads of the crowded cattle, the myriad muzzles and ears, the surge of energy, Joe was reminded of the ocean when it was choppy. He thought he knew why Overstreet was being so helpful.

Joe put his hot horse in a stall out of the wind and gave him a healthy ration of oats, which roared out of the bucket into the tin-lined trough. The little gelding always looked like he was falling asleep while he ate, and Joe watched him a moment before going out to check his gates.

Joe had become so preoccupied with getting the cattle shipped that his communications with Astrid almost came to a stop. She seemed to sense something and they rather politely stayed out of each other's way.

They loaded the cattle in the morning by the yard light. The metal loading chute rocked and crashed under their running weight. Joe went inside the trailer to help swing the partitions against the crowded animals. Their bawling deafened him. At the end of each load, the rope was released from the pulley and the sliding aluminum door flew down to a silent stop in the manure.

The first truck pulled off while the second one loaded. There were three frozen-footed steers that were crippled and hard to load. They went up last and the two trucks pulled out, their engines straining in low gear at the vast contents of living flesh going down the ranch road in bawling confusion. From beneath the bottom slats, the further green evidence of their terror went on flowing. Joe watched the back of the trailers rocking from side to side with the mass and motion of big trawlers in a seaway. In a moment, the red taillights had curved down past the cottonwoods and disappeared.

By three that afternoon, the cattle went through the sale at seventy-one and a half dollars a hundredweight and the money was sent to Lureen's account in Deadrock. And of course the ranch was Joe's. Mainly, it filled in the blanks in the painting of the white hills. A homeowner, a man of property. He sat in the living room with the deed in his lap. He showed it to Astrid. He fanned himself with it. He tried to make it a joke, but she didn't laugh and neither did he. He wondered what Smitty would do with the money.

Sometime after midnight, Joe was awakened from sleep by someone knocking on the door. Once he saw the clock and knew how late it was, he was filled with sharp panic. He got up without turning on the lights and eased into the kitchen. In the window of the door, he could see the shape of someone standing. He thought first of not answering the door and then wondered if it might not be a traveler, someone with car trouble, or a sick neighbor. And so he went into the kitchen and turned the light on. The minute he did that, the figure outside the door was lost. He opened the door on the darkness and said, "What is it?"

There was no reply. Joe had made out the shape of the figure. It looked like his father. The glow from the yard light, so recently cloudy with insects, was sharply drawn on the cold night. Joe wanted to say, "It's a clean slate." Surely this was a dream. It must have been a traveler.

Joe closed the door as quietly as he could but left it un-locked. There was no sound anywhere. He went back to bed and lay awake. He felt the cold from the blackened window over the bed. He had begun to suspect that by coming here at all, he had taken back his name. He remembered the sense of paralysis having a particular name had given him in the first place. He had loved moving into a world of other people's names. He had even tried other names and had felt a thrill like that of unfamiliar air terminals and railway stations, places where he could abandon himself to discreet crowd control. Finally, this took such vigilance it was wearying. He wanted his own name. And yet, the ride home through spring storms, through unfamiliar districts, had a quality that was independent of where he was coming from and where he was going. He had a brief thrill in thinking that all of life was about two things: either move or resume the full use of your name. But the idea slipped away when he tried to grasp it.

It was still dark when he got in the truck and filled it up at the fuel tank next to the barn. Then he began to drive. He drove to White Sulphur Springs, Checkerboard, Twodot, Judith Gap, Moccasin, Grassrange, Roundup, and home, four hundred miles without stopping.

By the time Joe pulled up in front of the house, he was exhausted. The lights shone domestically in the dark, illuminating parts of trees and the white stones of the driveway. It seemed that a placid, sunshot existence must be passing within.

Joe opened the door and Ivan Slater rose inelegantly from the deep, slumped couch while Astrid, standing a certain distance from one undecorated wall, tried to hang the moon with a smile that was both radiant and realistic.

"What are you doing here?" Joe demanded. "Where did you come from?" He smelled a rat. Ivan had been called in as Astrid's chief adviser before.

"Joe." She may have said something before that but Joe didn't hear it. Then she said, "I need to talk to you."

"I know," Joe said, noticing that whatever was in the air suspended Ivan's promotional bearing so that he stood exactly where he had arisen, taking up room. It was exactly the moment one would ordinarily say, "Stay out of this."

"Joe, let me run this by you," said Ivan. "Astrid isn't suited for this, somehow. She has asked me to help her get resituated. I'm Astrid's friend and this is what friends are for. P.S. We're not fucking."

"That's fine, I hate her," said Joe experimentally.

"Now Joe," Ivan said, "you've had a long drive."

"You knew I wouldn't stay," Astrid said. "What's this about, anyway? I don't know. But I do know I'm getting out of here. And it's a joke to claim you hate me."

"The fucking Cuban geek," Joe offered.

"Punch him in the nose, Ivan," said Astrid.

"That will do," Ivan said to Joe without emphasis.

"Take the dog with you," said Joe to Astrid. "That's the worst dog I ever saw. It'll be perfect for your new home."

"Okay, but don't generalize about me. And what is this about a new home?"

"I used to like dogs," Joe explained maladroitly.

"I had a lot to offer. I still do. Not for you, obviously. But who does? All I need to know is that it's not me. And I loved you. So, good luck. Good luck with the place. All the luck in the world with the cows. Enjoy yourself with the land. Happy horses, Joe."

"*I used to like women!*"

"I'm not like that dog, Joe," Astrid said.

"Don't jump to conclusions. I want you both out of here right away. I need a quiet place to sleep."

"Joe, it's late," Ivan said. "You're not in your right mind. As if you ever were, in fact."

"This advisory role you cultivate, Ivan, is unwelcome just now. I dislike having my time wasted."

"You're not that busy," sang Ivan. Joe sighed and looked at the floor. He wanted to collect his thoughts and he feared a false tone entering the proceedings. He wanted to leave off on a burnishing fury and empty out the house. It was hard to see that he'd had the intended effect; Ivan was scratching his back against the doorjamb. Astrid was smiling at a spot in midair. She was a fine girl. They had feared all along that they couldn't survive a real test. It had been lovely, anyway. It was a provisional life.

While they packed Astrid's things, Joe watched T V. As luck would have it, it was a feature on farm and ranch failures with music by Willie Nelson and John "Cougar" Mellencamp. He remembered leaving the deed in the truck. He might have left the windows open. Pack rats could get in and eat the deed. The wind could get the deed.

They came into the living room with their suitcases.

"This is pretty interesting. It's about farm and ranch failure," Joe said. "Can you go during the commercial?"

"No," said Astrid, "we're going now. Were you serious about that dog?"

"What next!" said Joe without taking his eyes off the screen.

"May I see you a moment, Joe?" Astrid stood in the doorway to their bedroom. Ivan studied the backs of his fingernails in the open front door, buffing them occasionally on his left coat-sleeve. Joe met Astrid in the bedroom and she shoved the door shut. She gave him a long look and took a deep breath.

"Let me tell you something, sport," she began, "you don't fool me with this tasteless display we've just witnessed."

"I don't."

"No, you don't."

"What sort of display would have struck you as less taste-less?"

"A sincere remark or two about your plight. A word of hope that you'll come to life soon. Your life."

"All whoppers!"

"I'm just gonna step back, and let you choose."

She went out the door. Joe followed her. Ivan was still in the same spot. When Joe went over, Ivan deployed his hand as a kind of handshake option, Joe's choice. Joe shook.

Ivan and Astrid went into the night. He heard them call the dog and when he saw the lights wheel and go out, and he knew the dog was gone, he at last realized how blithely things were being taken away from him. He went to bed and contained himself as well as he could, but the pillowcase grew wet around his face.

His sleep produced the need for sleep, for rest, for deep restoration from this masquerade of sleep in which all the tainted follies had opportunity for festivity and parade. He had Astrid in his arms and his inability to distinguish love and hate no longer mattered because she wasn't there in the light of day.

The cool spell passed and it was hot again. Joe was going to take a good long look at the white hills. He was going to start at the beginning. He got in the truck and drove toward the drought-ravaged expanses east of town where the road looked like a long rippled strip of gray taffy; on the farthest reaches of the road, looking as small as occasional flies, were the very few vehicles out today. Dust followed a tractor as an unsuccessful crop was plowed into the ground. Joe could picture the cavalry crossing here, following the Indians and their ghost dogs. Sheep were drifted off into the corners of pastures waiting for the cool of evening to feed. Ribbed cattle circled the tractor tires that held the salt. Old stock ponds looked like meteor craters and the weeds that came in with the highway gravel had blossomed to devour the pastures. It was neither summer nor fall. The sky was blue and the mountains lay on the horizon like a black saw. A white cloud stood off to one end of the mountains. In a small pasture, a solitary bull threw dust up under himself beneath the crooked arm of a defunct sprinkler. The thin green belt beneath the irrigation ditches contrasted immediately with the prickly pear desert that began inches above. The radio played "Black roses, white rhythm and blues." Astrid used to say, "I thought Montana was so unlucky for you. I can't understand why you want to go back." And he had said with what seemed like prescience and laudable mental health, "Yes, but I'm not superstitious!" And she'd said, "Wait a minute. You were pretty clear on this. You said it was unlucky for you and it was unlucky for everybody else."

Joe said, "That's my home!"

He stopped the truck at the bottom of a long, open draw and walked for almost an hour. At the end of that walk, he reached the gloomy, ruined, enormous house that he had long ago visited with his father, the mansion of the Silver King, a piece of discarded property no longer even attached to a remembered name. It was a heap out in a pasture and if you had never been inside it the way Joe had and felt in the design of its chambers the anger and assertion of the Silver King himself, the mansion didn't look good enough to shelter slaughter cattle until sale day. Grackles jumped and showered in the lee of its discolored walls and the palisade of poplars that led from the remains of the gate seemed like the work of a comedian.

Joe walked to the far side of the building and sat down close to the wall out of the wind. The mud swallows had built their nests solidly up under the eaves and wild roses were banked and tangled wherever corruption of the wall's surface gave them a grip. Concentric circles in the stucco surrounded black dots where stray gunfire had intercepted the building, adding to the impression that it was a fortress. Joe thought about how his father's bank had repossessed the property. His father was gone—even the bank was gone! He was going to go in.

A piece of car spring in the yard made a good pry bar, and Joe used it to get the plywood off one of the windows, leaving a black violated gap in the wall. He made a leap to the sill, teetering sorely on his stomach, then poured himself inside. He raised his eyes to the painting of the white hills.

Joe walked across the ringing flags to get a view of the picture. He could feel the stride the room induced and imagined the demands of spirit the Silver King made on everything. Such people, he thought, attacked death headlong with their insistence on comfort and social leverage. It was absolutely fascinating that it didn't work.

But the painting was still mysterious; it had not changed. "The only painting I've ever understood," said Joe's father after he had showed it to his son. "Too bad it's fading." The delicacy of shading in the overlapping white hills, rescued from vagueness by the cheap pine frame, seemed beyond the studied coarseness Joe's father leveled at everything else.

It was a matter of dragging an old davenport across the room and bracing it against one corner of the fireplace. He stepped up onto one arm, then to its back and then up onto the mantel. He turned around very slowly and faced the wall, to the left of the painting. By shuffling in slow motion down the length of the mantel he was able to move himself to its center.

There was no picture. There was a frame hanging there and it outlined the spoiled plaster behind it. It could have been anything. It was nothing, really. Close up, it really didn't even look like white hills. This of course explained why it had never been stolen. Joe concluded that no amount of experience would make him smart.

His father must always have known there was nothing there.

The rage Joe felt quickly ebbed. In his imaginary parenthood, he had begun to see what caused the encouragement of belief. It was eternal playfulness toward one's child; and it explained the absence of the painting. It wasn't an empty frame; it was his father telling him that somewhere in the abyss something shone.

He was driving a little too fast for a dirt road, tools jumping around on the seat of the truck and a shovel in the bed beating out a tattoo. He was going to see Ellen, sweeping toward her on a euphoric zephyr. He knew how intense he must look; and he began doing facial exercises as a preparation for feigning indifference. The flatbed hopped across the potholes. Antelope watched from afar. "Hi, kiddo," he said. "Thought I'd see how you were getting along." He cleared his throat and frowned. "Good afternoon, Ellen. Lovely day. I hope this isn't a bad time." He craned over so he could watch himself in the rearview mirror. "Hiya Ellen-baby, guess what? I'm gonna lose that fucking ranch *this week*. YAAGH!" A sudden and vast deflation befell him and he slumped in the front of the truck and slowed down. When he got to the schoolyard, the children were gone and Ellen was walking toward her old sedan in her coat.

She saw Joe and walked over toward him. She said, "Well, what do you know about that?"

"I wanted to see you," said Joe.

"Here I am."

"Have you been thinking?"

"About what? My phone bill? My cholesterol?"

"Your phone bill."

"I think about it every time I lift the Princess Touchtone to my ear. Incidentally, my husband and I are anxious for you to know how happy we are to have worked everything out. I realize I'm kind of repeating myself. But it seems we have to do that with you. Joe, I don't want to be this way."

"Can we take a short drive?" Joe asked.

"How short?"

"Five minutes."

"I guess it can be arranged," said Ellen and climbed in. Joe noticed how closely she followed the rural convention of going from an amorous interest to a display of loathing; in the country, no one broke off an affair amicably. Ellen looked out at the beautiful fall day, directing a kind of all-purpose disgust at falling aspen leaves. This was the sort of thing Astrid never put him through.

Joe drove back toward town and quickly approached its single stoplight; he was heading for the open country to show her the white hills, both the painting and the ones beyond, and explain enough about his life that he could, if necessary, close this chapter too.

"Where are we going?" Ellen asked in alarm. "Stop at this light and let me out." The light began to turn red. Ellen tried the door handle. Some pedestrians had stopped to look on. Joe ran the light. Ellen pushed the door open and shouted, "*Help!*" and Joe hit the gas. The bystanders fluttered into their wake. He watched in the rearview mirror as they started to go into action.

"We'll just take a little loop out toward the Crazies and I'll drop you back at the school. What in God's name caused you to yell that?"

"I wanted to be dropped off. Joe, you have to learn to take hints a little better than you do."

"I'm going to show you something and we're going to talk."

"About what? My husband and I are back together. We have resolved our differences. We're happy again. We're a god-damn couple, got it?"

"Why did you lie to me about Clara?"

She studied him for a moment in a shocked way. Then he saw she wouldn't argue.

"Billy and I had hit this rough spot in the road."

"I still don't follow you."

"It was Daddy's idea actually. He had worked it out on the calendar. I have to admit, it wasn't that far-fetched. But he's got that big bite missing from his ranch and he kind of put two and two together."

"You ought to be ashamed of yourself."

"Whatever." She turned to him suddenly. She made little fists and rolled her eyes upward. "You don't need to under-stand me. Billy knows everything there is to know about *me*, and he loves *me*."

Joe wished he had time to think about this. She had a point. It was about lives that were specific to each other. It wasn't about generalities. It wasn't about "love." "Love" was like "home." It was basic chin music.

Joe drove along slowly, as though adding speed would only substantiate the appearance of kidnap. Since he was pouring with sweat, he now merely wished to add a few amiable notes and get Ellen back to the schoolyard. This had all turned into something a bit different from what he had hoped for. At that very moment, he began to realize how much he wished he had Astrid advising him right now. She would say something quite concrete like "Hit the brakes" or "Don't do anything stupid. That way nobody will get hurt."

"Here they come," said Ellen.

"Here comes who?"

"Look in the mirror."

A small motorcade had formed a mile or so back; a cloud of dust arose from them and drifted across the sage flats. Joe picked up speed but couldn't seem to widen the gap. Perspiration broke out on his lip. "Are you going to clear this business up with that mob, if they catch us?"

"Let me get back to you on that," said Ellen with the faintest smile. Ellen had become so strange. It was more than indifference — it was a weird fog. He imagined her thinking how badly she wanted to get shut of this jackass and back to the husband and daughter she loved. This perception reduced Joe's account to virtual sardine size. He felt too paltry to go on taking the wheel.

He flattened the accelerator against the floor. The truck seemed to swim at terrific speed up the gradual grade toward the hills. A jack rabbit burst onto the road ahead of them, paced the truck for fifty yards and peeled off into the sagebrush. Nothing Joe did seemed to extend the distance between himself and the cluster of vehicles behind.

"Have you been doing any fishing?" Ellen asked.

"I really haven't had the time."

The truck skidded slightly sideways.

"Somebody said there's a Mexican woman staying with you." So that was it. A bird dove at the windshield and veered off in a pop of feathers.

"An old girlfriend," Joe said candidly. "It's a very sad thing. She couldn't stick it out. She'd had enough, and she was very patient in her own way. If she'd lied to me more I'd be with her today."

Ellen mused at the rocketing scenery.

"I've got a teacher's meeting in Helena," she said wearily. "On Tuesday. That's another world."

"Who will substitute for you?"

"An old lady who doesn't make the kids work. It makes me look like a bum." Somehow, Joe got the truck into a wild slide going down a steep grade into a gully. The truck turned backward at about sixty miles an hour. "This is really making me moody," said Ellen. They plunged into a grove of junipers and burst out the other side in a shower of wood and branches. Some of the foliage was heaped up against the windshield and it was a little while before Joe could see where he was going. The vigilantes were still bringing up the rear in a cloud of dust. One of them dropped back, a plume of steam jetting from the radiator.

It was hopeless. He couldn't outrun them in this evil, weak farm truck. All he wanted was a brainless chase that could last for weeks. He stopped, backed and turned around. Deadrock was visible in the blue distance. The machines advanced toward him. "You've really got a bee in your bonnet," Ellen said.

"Shut up, you stupid bitch, you rotten crumb."

"I *see*," said Ellen. "The idea being that I got you into this?"

Joe said nothing.

"After the big rush, I am now a 'stupid bitch.' This may be the first serious conversation we've had since we met. Are you telling me that it is possible I could mean more to you than pussy or golf lessons? Let's have it, Joe. I could actually rise in your esteem to the status of 'stupid bitch.' Oh, this *is* romantic. I had really misjudged the depth of feeling around here. And I've gone back to my husband when I could have enjoyed these passionate tongue-lashings."

At the approach of massed cars and trucks, Joe just stopped. Twenty vehicles wheeled all around them and skidded to a halt, dumping a small crowd of armed civilians, the State Farm agent, a mechanic still in his coveralls, a pharmacist in a white tunic of some kind, a couple of waitresses. They were still pouring out and a few guns had been displayed, when Ellen threw open her door and cried, "This is all a terrible misunderstanding! It was supposed to be a joke!" She climbed out of the truck. One of the mechanics, in coveralls and a gray crewcut that showed the crown of his head, came to the truck and held a gun to Joe's temple. Joe looked over to see Billy Kelton emerging from a Plymouth Valiant he should have recognized. "A complication," Joe said. "Here comes Billy."

"Son," said the man in the crewcut in a startlingly mild voice, "this is where she all comes out in the wash." Joe had a sudden feeling of isolation as Ellen walked over and joined her husband at a distance from the cluster of people and vehicles. Billy shoved her away from him and began to walk toward Joe's truck. Joe wondered what the shoving meant, in terms of a margin of safety, of an exploitable ambiguity.

"That's Billy," said Joe's guard. "He's getting ready to have a fit."

"What's he going to do?"

"Do? He's going back to Vietnam!"

The mechanic smiled like a season ticket holder. The blood beat in Joe's face. Joe thought that was the time to grab the gun but he just thought about it with a kind of longing, knowing he wouldn't have any idea what to do with it.

Billy came over with a bakery truck driver at his side, a blond-haired man with long sideburns and an expression of permanent surprise. "Something to tell the grandchildren, ay?" Billy said to the mechanic. "Get him out for me, would you?"

The mechanic opened the door and dragged Joe out. He and the man from the bakery held his arms, shoving him up against the car. Billy got so close, Joe could only focus on one of his eyes at a time. But it was enough for Joe to recognize that Billy didn't have his heart in this. Twice he had punched Joe years ago and apparently that was enough. "Time is hastening, Joe. You need to cut it out." Billy turned and spoke to the others. "You guys can go." They hesitated in their disappointment. "Go on," he said more firmly. They began to move off. "The show is over," he said, making what Joe considered an extraordinary concession.

"Is that it?" asked the mechanic.

"That's it," said Billy without turning back. "Ellen, take my car back to the house."

"He really didn't do anything, Billy."

"Probably not. Just go on back now with Vern and them."

Ellen moved away from them. A breeze had come up and the clouds were moving overhead rapidly. The air was cold enough that the exhaust smell of the vehicles was sharp. Billy turned to Joe once more. "We'll just let Ellen go on back to town with Vern and them. If she goes, they'll all go. They're upset because they couldn't lynch you. You and your family sure been popular around here. All them boys banked with your dad."

"Which one is Vern?" asked Joe without interest.

"Fella with the flattop."

"Oh." Joe's eyes drifted over to Vern, who was returning reluctantly to a car much too small for him. Joe couldn't see how he could even get in it. But he elected not to report this impression.

"Let me drive," said Billy, opening the door to get in. Joe slid over.

"The keys are in it," Joe said with a sickly smile.

Billy was wearing old levis and wingtip cowboy boots nearly worn through on top by spur straps. He smiled at Joe and started up the truck. Joe could see that the cars and trucks which had followed them were almost out of sight now. As the various members of the community who had come out to help returned to town in their cars, something went out of the air. Joe said, "I saw on the news they're having a potato famine in Malibu."

"I don't have too good a sense of humor today, Joe."

They drove on, and Billy was a careful driver. They took the road that went around to the south, which eventually connected to the ranch. "Am I the biggest problem you've got, Joe?" They both followed with their eyes a big band of antelope the truck had scared, all quick-moving does except for one big pronghorn buck who rocked along behind in their dust cloud.

"Not really."

Billy sighed. Joe looked out the windshield but saw nothing. Joe remembered one time he and Astrid were dancing to the radio and she called him "sweetheart." She had never called him that before and never did again. Everything takes place in time, Joe thought, wondering why that always seemed like such a heartbreaking discovery.

Suddenly, Joe wanted to talk. "My old man used to say, 'If

you ain't the lead horse, the scenery never changes.' Now it looks like I might lose the place. I need to get out front with that lead horse. I feel like I've been living in a graveyard."

Billy looked at him. Joe watched Billy deeply consider whether or not the fraternization was appropriate. It was clear that there was insufficient malice in the air to warrant this drive on any other basis. What a day we're having here, thought Joe.

After a resigned sigh, Billy started to talk: "When I come home, I pretty much come home to nothing. Except that we already had a kid. And then we got married. Old man Overstreet never let me forget I come into the deal empty-handed, just had my little house. He always introduces me, 'This here's my son-in-law Billy. He runs a few head of chickens over on the Mission Creek road about two and a half miles past the airport on the flat out there.' Never *will* let me forget. And I ought to punch you but I can't really. Life used to be so simple."

It was a long way around. It seemed as if the mountains toward Wyoming stayed the same size ahead of them, sharp shapes that curved off toward the Stillwater. You could be under traveling clouds and off toward the mountains the clouds would seem stopped. And the mountains looked like a place you'd never reach. On top of that, nobody seemed to want to get there much anyway. Billy must have felt Joe look over because he turned on the radio only to get the feverish accordion of Buckwheat Zydeco shouting out the bright nights of New Orleans. He turned it off and said, "I want to go back to work."

It seemed to Joe to be the most glowing of all thoughts. It went with the day and it went with their situation.

"I don't seem to understand what it means to have something," Joe said. "I don't seem to get what I ought to out of it. I feel like that place still belongs to my dad."

"It ought to belong to whoever's been working on it."

"Which is you, I suppose."

"It was when Overstreet had it leased. When you took it back, I had to go up to the house. That was when me and Ellen started to have such a wreck. We ain't over it yet. We may never get over it. She was raised up to think I ought to have something, and I don't." Joe remembered long ago when Billy had punched him out at the railroad station, and he thought he might have understood even then how the dispossessed are quick with their fists. But now Billy seemed to have lost even that capability. Joe thought that at the narrow crossroads in which Billy Kelton lived, the use of his hands had been cruelly confined to a kind of unchosen service. Lack of his own ground indentured him to people smaller than himself.

"That place of mine," Joe said, "has got serious debt against it but a man who wanted to stay and fight it ought to be able to hang on to it." He stared at the beautiful prairie and wondered if anyone had ever owned it. "I don't want to stay and fight it. That's just not me."

Billy slowed the truck. "Have you seen my father-in-law's map?"

"The one with the missing piece?"

"Do you have any idea what it would mean if I had that little chunk of the puzzle? Even for five minutes?"

"I probably don't," said Joe. "But we're all so different."

35

Joe had dinner with Lureen at her house. She didn't feel like cooking, so Joe stopped off for some chicken, a carton of cole slaw, and some soft drinks. She greeted him in the doorway, then went right back inside and sat under the kitchen window with her hands in her lap. Looking at her, Joe wondered if it wouldn't be the kindest thing he could do to burn her house down.

Joe walked around opening cupboards, looking for dishes and utensils and glasses, then set the kitchen table for the two of them. He got Lureen to come over and they sat down to eat. She didn't seem to want to eat much. Joe bit into a drumstick, then watched her over the top of it while he chewed. He tried the cole slaw. It was sweet and creamy like a dessert.

"Good chicken," he said.

"Delicious."

"You haven't tasted it yet."

"I will. Thank you for bringing it."

"Look at it this way," said Joe. "It's not beef! Ha-ha!" She took it in listlessly. A bird hit the window and they both looked up.

"It's all right," said Joe. "Didn't hit that hard."

Then he noticed Lureen's tears falling in the cole slaw.

"You must have foreseen this," he said.

"I didn't, Joe."

He chewed on the drumstick, trying to have a perception.

"But didn't it ring kind of a bell after it happened?"

"No."

"It was a bit of a crooked scheme for all parties concerned," Joe pointed out, actually enjoying this store chicken.

"*I know!*" Lureen wailed, throwing herself back in her chair.

"Long ago, my father, your brother, your *other* brother, told me never to take my eyes off Smitty."

"It's going to be hard to watch him in Hawaii," Lureen sniveled with an extraordinary, crumpled misery that Joe had not only never seen before in her but never seen in anyone of her age.

The phone rang and Joe answered it. The lovely and cultivated voice of a young woman explained that he, as the head of the household, was a finalist in a multi-million-dollar sweepstake. Joe cut her off. "I'm not the head of a household," Joe said and went back to Lureen.

"Wrong number," he said.

"Was it those sweepstakes people?"

"Yes."

"They're used to speaking with Smitty," she said and began to cry again. Joe's heart ached to see his poor little aunt in this condition even if she had brought it upon herself. He could see a tulip glow from the setting sun high in the kitchen windows. And then the perception came.

"Lureen, I'm going to tell you something and I want you

to listen carefully." She stared at him like a child. "You know our Smitty," he said and she nodded her head up and down in a jittery fashion. "He'll spend all that money. You know that and I know that." He let this sink in. "And it won't take long." The nodding stopped. She was listening raptly. Joe was now ready to drop the panacea. *"And then he'll be back."*

Lureen stopped all motion. She looked at Joe's face with extraordinary concentration.

"Are you telling me the truth?"

"Yes."

"And it won't take that long?"

"Not that long at all."

"I ask myself if he's really secure in Honolulu. You read from time to time of racial problems there. The Hawaiians are quick to throw a punch and they are absolutely enormous."

And it's unrealistic to expect another thorough bombing by the Japanese, Joe thought. Lureen picked up a wing and seemed to admire it. "You're one hundred percent right about his inability to handle his finances," Lureen observed in a comparatively lusty voice. "I might just as well start resigning myself to the reappearance of his little face at the screen."

"Not a moment to lose," said Joe tonelessly. "Start resigning yourself today." He gave her a confirming gesture with his bare drumstick which was reminiscent of the heads of corporations Ivan admired so, the ones who promoted their own products on television. Then he looked up to the band of sky in the window. He had seen that band when his grandfather died and he had asked his grandmother if he'd left him any gold.

As the principal lien-holder, Darryl took in hand the matter of working out the closing, the ritual exchange of a dollar bill so crumpled it took two paper clips to attach it to the documents. Joe accepted that the substitution of a born-to-the-soil type like Billy Kelton for a drifter like himself was equal in favorable impact to keeping it out of the hands of an opportunistic schemer like Overstreet who never borrowed from banks anyway. The picture of this hard-working cowboy with an honorable service record holding a gun to Overstreet's head would be applauded throughout the community and give them something to discuss other than the *Dead End* sign the state had put up on the road into the cemetery. Overstreet paid Joe one visit, waving a checkbook and making one or two ritual threats which were windier than his usual succinct style. It had been years since Joe had heard the phrase "rue the day" and he mulled it over until the words dissolved into nonsense.

The mineral rights were briefly a hitch. Joe couldn't at first face that his father had long ago placed them in trust for a caddies' college fund in Minnesota. But when he realized this, he knew finally that his father had really said goodbye to the place even before his soul left his body in that four-door Buick. He borrowed Darryl's phone at the bank while the principals still sat around the contracts in a cloud of cigarette smoke, and called Astrid to explain his latest theory, that they could work it out. Astrid's reply was typical, almost vintage, Astrid.

He drove toward the ranch that was no longer his. It was hard not to keep noticing the terrific blue of the autumn sky. The huge cottonwoods along the river had turned purest yellow, and since no wind had come up to disturb the dying leaves, the great trees stood in chandelier brilliance along the watercourses that veined the hills. Joe had to stop the truck to try to take in all this light.

The branches were heavy with early wet snow. Joe looked out from his kitchen window and felt his unshaven face. The light on the snow-edged world was dazzling. He used to feel this way a lot, almost breathless. He quickly started a pot of coffee and returned to the window to look at the snow starting to shrink in the morning sun. There was a soft mound of it on his woodpile, and on the ends of the logs he could see that water from snow melt had sunk into the wood. A sudden memory came back across the years: his father cleaning grouse at the sink in the ranch kitchen, a raft of feathers on darkened water. "I wish I was a vegetarian," he'd laughed. "You never have to pick number-eight shot out of a tomato!" The sky was blue and the air coming from under the slightly opened window so cool and clean that he admitted to himself that his spirits were starting to soar. He thought he'd begin to get his things together. He stood in the window a moment more and looked out at the beautiful white hills.

What Astrid had said, more or less, was that they would pretty much have to see.